SHERLOCK HOLMES & THE SINGULAR AFFAIR

SHERLOCK HOLMES &
THE SINGULAR AFFAIR

M. K. WISEMAN

ISBN: 978-1-7344641-3-9 (hardcover)

ISBN: 978-1-7344641-4-6 (paperback)

ISBN: 978-1-7344641-5-3 (ebook)

This is a work of fiction. Any references to real people, places, or historical events are used fictitiously. Other names, characters, places, descriptions, and events are products of the author's imagination or creations of Sir Arthur Conan Doyle and any resemblances to actual places or events or persons, living or dead, is entirely coincidental.

Edited by MeriLyn Oblad

Cover Illustration by Egle Zioma

Interior design created with Vellum

Published in the United States of America

1st edition: December 7, 2021

mkwisemanauthor.com

Contents:

FOREWORD

By Dr. J. Watson:

The story laid before you entered my possession shortly after the passing of my friend, Mr. Sherlock Holmes. Though The War and life in general had endeavoured to come between us in the years following our departure from Baker Street, one might say that our partnership remained eternal, a thing which no amount of space or time could sunder. I wish I could claim that now. The permanent separation which yawns before me puts even the three-year horror of The Great Hiatus into a different light. Then, I had no inkling that the man would return to us. Now, I know he cannot.

In his retirement he had accomplished what he had long threatened: Sussex Downs and honey bees, monographs and—I am sure—no small amount of boredom. But not the sort of boredom, however, which previously had driven Holmes to certain chemical excitations or suppressions of mind. This I judged from the lack of apparatus for such amongst his things.

No, the paraphernalia of the great man's life had reduced itself to a rich broth of experience, memory, intellect, and comfort. He had a great many books. The indexes, containing criminal data going back decades, were sent to the Yard. I can only pray that they see the value of their contents and preserve them.

To me, John Watson, chronicler and friend, he left an old tin box. Large-ish but otherwise unre-markable in appearance to anyone save myself, I knew its incalculable wealth from a conversation he and I had once had in front of the hearth at 221 on a cold winter's night.

Red tape bundles of paper and other curiosities lay nestled within that chest. Case notes. Many from the time before I had known him. It was here the enormity of the loss—that of the world and mine—caught me afresh while I thumbed through the worn pages, and I had to look away from the all-too-familiar handwriting to blink a tear from my eye.

At length I returned to my task and saw that lying conspicuously amongst its fellows was some-thing recent. Something new. My publishers would hardly call it a manuscript. But there it was. Type-written and done up with a bit of twine. He had tacked a letter to the front of it. It was addressed to me:

"My dear Watson," he said, "I find in these long and sunny afternoons that a certain nostalgic fever sweeps over my mind. This same malady seems to have affected my fingers and wrists, reaching even to my inkpot and pen. (I claim an application of artistic licence here, for you can see that a typewriter has been employed in the setting down of some of that which follows.)

" 'Why this case? Why now?' I know you are asking these questions, Watson. I have asked them myself. The application of word to page has never been my forte. But when the muse demands, I can see well that one must listen. How you could labour under the forceful direction of such a siren for so long astonishes and flatters me all the more.

"I can only hope that I may finish in time. If you are reading this letter, then you will already know what time I anticipate. Thus, I direct your attentions to the Singular Affair of the Aluminium Crutch and remain, my dear fellow,

"Very sincerely yours,
    "Sherlock Holmes"

A NON-MISSING MISSING
PERSONS CASE

CHAPTER 1

"Oh, but, Mr. Holmes, you must understand. That man. The man claiming to be Tobias-Henry Price, the man who everyone—who the world—believes to be Tobias-Henry Price . . . is not my fiancé!"

It had promised from the first to be a simple missing person case. Hand-wringing and blinked-back tears from my potential client, her well-meant worry, these had their place within my day-to-day intellectual exercises, often shelved somewhere between "monotonous" and "trite" in my mental bookshelves. Her story ran along familiar lines: Letters exchanged for months, fervent promises for a far shorter period of time. A meeting, a deferment. And then?

As I had just finished telling Miss Eudora Frances Clarke—the young woman who sat atremble in the cane chair opposite my own—these types of situations often resolved themselves in a few days' time; a few weeks, if the man in question were a complete scoundrel.

But her protestation brought me up short, and I held back on a second disinterested reassurance and dismissal.

She raised her chin, seeing as I had not chosen to respond. Her eyes flashed as she said, "I am in my right mind as to the knowing of my childhood friend—my dearest friend in all the world outside of my late father. Even with a space of ten-odd years, I know Toby's manners, his patterns of speech, his . . . heart."

"And so the gentleman who you accosted on St. James's Street outside of his club—"

"Merely wears the name and reputation of my own Tobias-Henry."

"A costume that no less than twenty of the man's closest peers can attest to. A ruse perpetuated by your fiancé's words—did you not say that it was he who confirmed his club's location? His membership therein?"

"Yes. And Tobias' uncle. And my cousin. As I said, I stand against the world in my convictions as to the identity of the man I love."

"This leaves no other circumstance but to suggest that you've been made the victim of a cruel deception by one man rather than played the fool by a host of others, Miss Clarke."

"If that is the case, Mr. Holmes, I would then ask that you consider my problem not a question of who is using the name and status of my childhood friend so freely but, instead, return to my initial concern and the only one which truly matters.

What has become of the man with whom I have exchanged important promises of the heart? It remains that there is a man gone missing——"

"A mystery compounded by the very fact that he claims to be a person who is clearly not missing at all," I mused, sitting back in my chair.

"A mystery made more cryptic by the fact that there is nobody but myself to question why such sinister duplicity even exists."

"Yourself and . . . one other, Miss Clarke." I gave her my most comforting smile before steepling my fingers and half closing my eyes to listen. "From the beginning, then. Pray be as detailed as you can. Omit nothing."

I must admit, she had my curiosity roused. For all that the case was likely to have the simplest of solutions——and one which would leave Miss Clarke heartbroken but, I hoped, unruined——I was interested in seeing the untanglement of this particular knot. If only for the satisfaction of knowing what Miss Clarke's "Toby" was playing at, how exactly he had managed to come upon such particulars as would convince her of his assumed identity, and the chance that, at the case's conclusion, one more villain might be kept from villainy in the future.

I waited while my client composed herself once more. A slight pause and then, "Toby and I——you'll forgive my continued familiarity, Mr. Holmes, but with another man publicly using his name, I would rather be frank than inexact. As I have said, Toby and I grew up together. Not merely as close friends, no. His father and my own were as brothers, in arms and in sentiment. Both served abroad, and when the time came, both chose to raise his family in the far-flung reaches wherein they found themselves. Sadly, Toby's father met his end at the claws of a tiger before the boy had reached the age of five. My mother, she passed of a fever which swept through the regiment when I was seven. Toby and his mother came to live with us after that, but alas, no further union was made between his family and mine. Four years later, Toby's mother succumbed to illness, and he was sent to his uncle in Norfolk. Sir Edgar Price. Though a man of some reputation and wealth, he was considered an eccentric—Toby's words, not mine, Mr. Holmes. A reclusive bachelor, he took Toby in as the son he never had.

"There were letters. At first. Toby and I became inconsistent correspondents, he telling me of his studies and his uncle's fearsome temper and I responding with stories of people and places we had known together. I—" Miss Clarke's voice faltered, and she looked downward to where her fingers had taken to fidgeting with her handkerchief. A moment later her clear-eyed gaze met mine, and she continued. "I had hopes, of course. My father, too. But then all communication ceased. I worried. I eventually wrote to Toby's uncle and was informed that Mr. Price was abroad on business, and he would write to me if he saw fit to. The impudence of my inquiry was all but stated in that letter."

Blushing, Miss Clarke put a hand to her cheek, the memory of Sir Edgar's censure still burning brightly in her face.

"You and Mr. Price's uncle do not get along, then."

"I cannot quarrel with a man whom I have never met," Miss Eudora Clarke gave her careful answer. She then continued, giving in to the guileless judgment which she had so far demonstrated in her more feeling parts of our interview. "I can say from Tobias-Henry's letters that his uncle never intended anything save the best for his only nephew and intended heir."

"But?"

"We all have tempers, Mr. Holmes." She gave a crooked, pained smile. "Toby was—is—a man who resembles his uncle in that one particular. Oh, not that he is cruel, no. As a boy he was the sweetest, kindest of souls. But he has within him a certain wildness of spirit. There were hints in his letters to me that not everything he did was"—Miss Clarke lowered her voice—"above board."

"And so you worry for him not merely because a man you regard has gone missing under unusual circumstances but out of other, potentially more sinister, fears."

"Yes, Mr. Holmes."

"And you stand completely firm in your conviction that your Toby and the missing man are one and the same."

"Yes!"

"Then it is a worry to be heeded. Please, continue. You came to England . . . ?"

"Three months back. To attend to my cousin who has been ill."

"And your letters with Mr. Price had become frequent once more."

"For almost two years, yes. He had returned

home, and in his letters he now made promises. Promises for our future. I had but to stay where I was and remain faithful to our dream, and he would soon join me. His duties to his uncle were ending; his future, secure."

"But you came here."

"Yes, and for it, we quarrelled. At Twayside. A fearful row. Toby was furious that I should have come upon him so unexpectedly. His uncle's temper and sense of propriety run within his makeup, too. To Toby's mind, to settle in the neighbourhood of his uncle was to reveal to Sir Edgar—to society— our romantic intents, something for which Toby was not yet prepared."

Particularly considering that another man occupied that very public position, I mused.

"Believe me when I tell you that I, too, have examined and then vehemently dismissed such a possibility as my being out of my senses." She laughed, a strangled noise which bordered on hysterics. "I could have writ the whole experience off as my being played the fool but for that I know what I know and so cannot make the math come out right in my mind. It makes me uneasy. It makes me uneasy, Mr. Holmes, to know that my Toby has a minute scar below his right eye. Just there. From a minor accident when he was eight. I tended him, Mr. Holmes. It makes me uneasy to realize that this man, who I believe I know, keeps my likeness upon his watch chain next to a ring I gave him on the occasion of our first parting seventeen years back."

"Nobody is questioning whether you saw what you say you saw. I am, in fact, grateful for your instincts in that they may serve to keep you from some danger."

"Danger, Mr. Holmes!" Again the threat of an emotional breaking point clouded my client's steady horizon. The handkerchief in her hand succumbed to helpless strangulation. Still she managed, "Where from?"

"You live in the country. Are there other houses nearby?"

"Saxlingham." She breathed the name. "And we are quite remote."

" 'We.' Your cousin, does she maintain staff?"

"Yes. My presence at Violet's side is but for the comfort which only family can provide. Twayside House stands alone but is not unguarded."

"That is gratifying to hear, Miss Clarke. You may expect me to come calling at the home of your cousin by Thursday at the latest." We both rose, and I accompanied Miss Clarke to the door.

TRITE TALK OF VIOLINS

CHAPTER 2

L et me first say, most emphatically, that curiosity does not a case make. In my experience, however, it may function much the same as hard evidence or fact. The human mind is particularly attuned to pattern, to its recognition and, thus, discernment of when said pattern is broken.

The source of Miss Clarke's troubling disparity as to the true identity of Mr. Price was likely not a large crime. It was, quite possibly, not a crime at all. But it was not nothing, and thus the very idea of the thing had awakened in my imagination a series of questions, and it was wholly within my power to discover the answers. And though no particular threat had been levelled at Miss Clarke, the menace of harm hung over her, and I should very much like to put that consideration to rest.

My first task following the interview with my new client was to confirm what I could of her story.

And so I set about determining the contours of truth and fact. In hunting about my over-crammed desk, I quickly discovered that my ticket for the Reading Room of the British Museum had lapsed into expiration and jotted off a quick note of application. So much for that avenue of research. Then again, what was my index for if not to provide me with easy reference at a moment's notice?

I glanced to the clock, debated pipe or coffee, and then chose neither.

My records on things military were so thin as to be essentially nil. It was to Edgar Price of Norfolk that I must look. I had lived at 59 Montague for long enough that various parts of my index had begun to spill out of their modest shelving to invade various parts of my living space. Crime could come from any quarter, and my commonplace books acted as a clearing house so that my mind could remain efficient, freed from jumbled, irrelevant facts. My collection of biographies currently resided by the foot of my bed, and I hurried to retrieve "P" from amongst my collection.

Sir Edgar Price. Born 1824 and the eldest of three children. The youngest, a sister, had died in infancy. The middle child had gone on to have an indifferent military career and one child—the now-missing Tobias-Henry. Sir Edgar's father had invested heavily in the railway game back in the '40s, thus securing his family's future fortunes. But Sir Edgar, bachelor and semi-permanent convalescent, had never married. His only heir was Mr. Tobias-Henry Price, consequence of his brother's predeceasing him and leaving the young man for Sir Edgar to rear.

Serendipitous speculation within the production and trade of aluminium at a time when the metal was precious and rare had furthered Sir Edgar's fortunes and earned him a fearsome reputation. Luckily the public at large was spared from his presence, as he had thrust his nephew into the social circles that he himself might have otherwise occupied.

Mr. Tobias-Henry Price would one day be a very wealthy man.

"However, from his address, I would gather that he is living under considerably more modest conditions at present. At least when he writes to Miss Clarke." Frowning, I eyed the paper upon which I had jotted Toby's town address. A good deal of my success as the world's only unofficial consulting detective came from my having made it my business to know every street, alleyway, and footpath in London. I had a precise working knowledge of the city and her surroundings, kept current via regular surveillance and study—itself a useful exercise, for an area's changing history had bearing on so many things.

Simply put: a gentleman of the Oaks Club did not strike me as the type to live at the far end of Noel Street.

Short minutes later, I lingered in front of Mr. Price's house, knowing without having to ring that it was empty or that its inhabitant wished it to appear so. I noted a few pertinent details and turned my steps onward to Pall Mall, mulling over

Miss Clarke's situation and the fact that I, too, was about to perform my own act of impudence in club-land. And with a member of society with whom one most definitely did not ever want to make an enemy of.

An expanse of fashion and exorbitance, of gossip and social jockeying, Pall Mall Street leading into St. James's seemed, to me, capable of producing a perfumed stink reaching higher and broader into the London skies than any of her more odoriferous industries. The district was, too, a haven, a quiet refuge for those privileged enough to be counted amongst the varied memberships. A place where one's opinion was echoed and magnified by adherents to the same ideas. Had Narcissus been a supporter of club life, he might have been found in some smoking room of St. James's, gazing contentedly into one of its mirrors.

Ah, the indolent "idleatry" of the rich and well-connected.

Technically, they were my lot. I had claim there if I wanted it. (I did not.) But they had their uses, these men who wanted to run the world—and, for better or worse, often did. For me and my work, it meant predictability, both in secrets and in crime.

And for one Langdale Pike, it meant for a steady income.

Seated centrally within the lineup of clubs, Mr. Pike enjoyed a commanding view from his bow window. A silent spider in the middle of society's web, he lay in wait, his ears open, eyes sharp, poised and attuned to the slightest vibrations: a hint of scandal, a whiff of *faux pas*.

He was not a blackmailer. Oh, no. Their kind I abhorred with every bone in my body. To my mind, bloody murder was cleaner than the evil by which a blackmailer made commerce.

No, Mr. Pike was a man who ensured that the societal rumour mills ran; his careful and diligent work providing a steady stream of the aforementioned scandals and lapses in propriety. And according to my sources, he was the very best. Thus his opinion on the legitimacy of Mr. Tobias-Henry Price was as good a starting place—or better—than any other I might try.

I passed the Oaks on my way to Mr. Pike's club and wondered if I should have luck enough to encounter Mr. Price. But no matter. I needed to build my case. Stone not sand, Sherlock. With that helpful reminder and a wry smile, I skipped up the steps to the Bagatelle.

Inquiring within, I found my quarry on the edge of escaping. The bow window seat sat vacant, recently abandoned by all indications. I fished in my pocket for a card only to have luck stay my hand. Mr. Pike himself came 'round the corner and allowed himself to be delayed for the introduction.

He was as his reputation suggested. Barrel-chested and broad-faced, Mr. Pike outfitted himself handsomely, though not ostentatiously so. He wore a well-brushed hat in the latest style, and on the last finger of his right hand I espied a serpentine ring with a dark, glittering stone. Small features both, but indicative of temperament and standing—

membership at the Bagatelle notwithstanding. Langdale Pike struck me as a man fastidious yet not scrupulous, confident but not brash. I could feel, instinctively, how secrets leached out of men's hearts in such a presence as his.

Langdale Pike grasped my hand, breaking into a wide smile as he caught my name. "Oh, I believe I can allow myself to be detained for yet a little while longer and enjoy the pleasure of your company, Mr. Holmes."

Indicating the newly reset window-side table, he moved off to reclaim his favoured perch. I followed, noting that he allowed me the better of the two chairs as regards to lighting. Interesting man. My return smile was genuine as I sat and faced him, the window overlooking the street to my right and the sparsely populated parlour of the Bagatelle Club open on my left.

Pike folded his hands on his lap and leaned forward over the small table. "Mr. Sherlock Holmes. I had an idea that you and I would cross paths one of these days. Come then. Tell me something about myself."

Offered without any sign of malice, the challenge was a test. My smiled faded, and I looked out the window to the passersby. I said, "Far be it from me to meet a man that many know from notoriety alone and proceed to make statements about him in an establishment such as this. Such impolite manners on my behalf would tell you more about me than I say about you.

"But I have been meaning to ask you one thing, Mr. Pike." I turned and gazed upon him. "If I could have the name of your luthier. Surely he must be accomplished and trustworthy, what with an instrument such as yours. A Guadagnini, is it?"

A pause. And then, Mr. Pike sat back in his seat, silent laughter making his big frame quiver. Lifting his hands, he laid one glove down upon the table, then tugged at the fingertips of the other. The garnet on his ring flashed with the motion. Left hand freed, he wriggled his fingers, thoughtfully touching his thumb to each callous.

I explained, "The hardened knob along your right index finger, just there. I noted it when we shook hands. More telling, however, is the patch of discoloured skin under your jawline along the left-hand side. Practice less and play more, perhaps, and you can avoid that detractor. And besides that, you yourself are not above inclusion in the paper every now and again."

A shock, a quickly put away ire replaced by the cool bemusement of complete self-assurance, flitted through Pike's features, and he waited the half second for my clarification. I chuckled and indulged, "I, too, am an enthusiast and saw you play—oh, it would have been seven, eight months back."

"I had no notion that our acquaintances ran in similar circles." The easy smile was back, and my companion shook his head. "Yes. That was me. Fauré's Berceuse. Opus 16—a sweet, lyrical little piece. You play, Mr. Holmes?"

"A little." I gave a quick, fleeting smile of acknowledgment. "But not as often or as with form enough to have had it leave its mark upon my chin.

In my line of work, I cannot afford tell-tale callouses."

"To that—" Pike lowered his voice, pausing so that he next spoke where there was a rise in the background noise of the room. "To that end, I must ask—bluntly—what it is that brings you here. Besides the obvious, of course. Trite talk of violins. You may find that is the only conversation I wish to have."

I followed his lead, waiting with my response so that my words would not carry over into silence. "I would not expect you should compromise yourself or anyone else with what you elect to say to me. Same as I presume discretion in any inquiry I bring to you."

He nodded.

"Tell me what you think of Mr. Tobias-Henry Price."

He raised his eyebrows. "Is this about that woman?"

"This is about what you think of Mr. Price." Here I was firm.

"What I think. Not what others do?" He leaned back. "He is a useless man. Dresses like a stage-door dandy, but I don't believe his morals allow him full access into that world."

"He has someone then?"

"No. He is a complete—rather I should say, an eligible—bachelor. His uncle dotes upon him. Indulges in any whim and fancy he takes to. Monetarily, that is." He turned from me and held up four fingers. He winked and said, "A year."

My, my. Miss Clarke had expensive tastes in scandal, I mused.

Pike continued, "He is reputed to be a kind, generous soul, with his merits far outweighing his faults, the latter being mainly composed of how he dresses and the freedom with which he spends his money. You cannot buy your way into the right position in society, but he would try. And then there is his uncle."

"Yes?" I leaned forward in my chair, a hound with the scent.

"He's abominable." Pike shrugged. "He will not leave his house and so sends his nephew 'round to fulfil social obligations. They are quite unalike, Mr. Price and Sir Edgar. As I say, Price is amiable. Sir Edgar . . . is not. In fact, Price handled the incident with the impudent young woman with grace and charm. One might say he was intrigued, even."

He waited. I said nothing, gave nothing.

He continued in a safer direction, "Mr. Tobias-Henry Price's club is the Oaks Club—for horse-racing enthusiasts, but really, who isn't?"

I snorted. Same could be said of Bagatelle Card Club. "Betting man?"

"Nothing formal, perhaps. But wagers on amateur sport are more the exception than the rule. I believe he prefers to ride. In fact he—" Pike cleared his throat and indicated with a nod of his head a man walking along the pavement opposite the club. "In fact, there is the gentleman himself."

Mr. Tobias-Henry Price appeared to be in a hurry, and so I was only able to form half an impression of the man. Tall and strikingly handsome, Mr. Price was not a man designed to blend in, an effect he furthered through his boisterous apparel.

"What's that then?" I indicated the cane in Price's hand. It flashed with each step he took, catching the bright afternoon sun and throwing it boldly back upon his fellow passersby.

Pike chuckled. "That would be Sir Edgar's famous aluminium crutch. Twenty years back, when it was made, it would have been worth a king's ransom, but now it's a mere curiosity. Part of the family fortune comes from the elder Price's speculating in the extraction and production of the metal, you understand. Said venture contributes in equal portion to Sir Edgar's reputation of having a bad humour—they say he is a good deal responsible for the initial scarcity of the material, controlling the chemical processes and developments so as to stoke the public fervour for the new metal. 'An iron fist wielding a gleaming aluminium cane.' Mr. Price became ward of his uncle at a tender age. I would not have liked to have been in the position of a young person growing up within that melancholy house. Not good for a body."

"As you say, Price has a reputation for kindness. Perhaps Mr. Price has usurped that symbol, adopting it to match his own glittering life," I countered, testing further.

Langdale Pike smiled. "Yes, but every man's story has within it a 'However . . .' as my own profession—and yours—will attest. The trick is in discovering it."

PITTED ONE AGAINST THE OTHER

CHAPTER 3

A nighttime sojourn to Noel Street provided for me two important pieces of information. For one, the house was indeed unoccupied and had likely been so for the duration suggested by Miss Clarke. As to the second, my gentle housebreaking to ascertain that first determination allowed me time enough to conclude that I was, at that point, the sole party interested in the empty home.

But I could not spend my days watching an empty residence of a man who had already been gone for weeks. And any leads I sent out into the darkness of London's underworld were not likely to bear fruit until more time had passed.

So I was to spend time in the light, learning what I could of our mysterious usurper: Mr. Tobias-Henry Price of the Oaks Club, St. James's Street.

Unfortunately, I feared that my own person did not gleam as brightly as time in Mr. Price's circle would require. I would have to leave myself behind. And, while it was easy to fall through the ranks of society with the introduction of a ragged coat, a changed gait, or an adopted malady to one's appearance, rising was decidedly difficult.

But all that would come later, after I had called upon both Toby's uncle and his worried fiancée. Thus I forwarded my things to one of the more annoyingly fashionable hotels and, myself, set off towards Norfolk.

The train ride to Sheringham was uneventful and my carriage ride to Holt even less so. It gave me ample time to reflect. I had begun my investigations on the premise that Miss Clarke was telling the truth. If she were in any real danger, that was the safest course to pursue. And if she lied? The truth of it would out.

The question remained: what crime was actually being committed here? Appearances pointed more and more to Miss Clarke's "Toby" being the villain—something I had suspected from the first. Yet if that man bore more personal resemblance to someone Miss Clarke had known all her life than he who wore the name publicly, the question of wrongdoing fell on the side of the man at the Oaks.

My impression of Sir Edgar Price might serve to answer many of my misgivings.

At least there were not two of him.

The reclusive uncle of Mr. Tobias-Henry Price lived just east of the village of Bodham, which made my pre-excursion to Holt something of a backwards manoeuvre. To call upon Sir Edgar without having first done away with the wrinkles and fatigue of my travels, however, would have put me at the disadvantage. I desired a good impression, for I desired candour from him.

I rang. I was admitted. There, in a cold but sumptuous parlour, I waited for the master of the house. A quick look around gave me a firm impression of the man's taste in artwork: requisite paintings plus some more worldly curiosities which sat high on a shelf but very pointedly on display. The air of the manor itself seemed strained, as though every occupant were in the habit of holding their breath, guilty like a child who had been caught in a misstep. The invisible pressure seemed to rob even the hall clock of its stately sound. The marking of the hour fell muted within the elegant furnishings. This was a house of secrets, no doubt. At length I heard a measured step and turned from my observations to greet Sir Edgar a moment later.

"Mr. Sherlock Holmes. Of London," this the master of the house said with a growl, levelling piercing eyes at me from under a heavy brow. His grizzled head hung low over his shoulders, and he stood stooped like some bird of prey. His hands he kept clasped behind him, and his legs quivered so that the rest of him shook as if with uncontainable fury or energy. While I knew the man to be in his fifties, Sir Edgar was aged beyond his years, the toll of decades of stress and emotional turmoil leaving his remaining sharpness and vitality to show through all the more for it. Langdale Pike's words returned to me, his lament that a child had had to grow up under the care of such a harsh, uncompromising person. For all that Sir Edgar posed no threat to me, I found something within me fearing him.

He noted where I stood and inclined his head, saying, "Have you any knowledge of the pottery and stone carving traditions of the Americas?"

I replied in the negative but complimented the little collection. Sir Edgar gave a non-verbal grunt and took several shuffling, trembling steps over to a stiff-looking chair where he sat heavily. He indicated its partner. "Well then, have a seat. Brandy? Whisky?"

I thanked him and applied for the latter.

"We will have our drink, stare daggers at one another, and then you will be on your way, Mr. Holmes." He lifted his glass and downed its contents. "There. Now you tell Miss Clarke that if my nephew wishes to pursue her, she will be second to know of it. Absent that, she should stay clear of him and his set."

I smiled at his presumptions behind my having called. If he were to as eagerly lay the rest of his potential guilt out for me, I should have an easy time of it. I said, "I believe that the incident where she confronted your nephew on St. James's was a simple case of mistaken identity—"

"And here? She mistook me, too? And in my own home? No, Mr. Holmes, you won't put me out like that."

"You know Miss Clarke? You've met her?" Surprise got the better of me. That was one lie tallied to her account, then.

"She has met me, yes. Pretty thing. Smart, too, if a bit too feeling for my tastes. But altogether an admirable specimen of her sex. As I said, Tobias is free to pursue her if he so chooses and not the other way around."

"Then you would not object to Miss Clarke for your nephew?"

"Ha! She is headstrong. Bold beyond propriety. But you've seen my nephew, I dare say." Those shrewd gimlet eyes were back on me, boring into me. "Or heard of him. A peacock, dancing close as he dares to the edges of what good society will quietly accept. Quite a pair they would make, yes? No, I would not object. I do not object. What I am is annoyed. Her impertinence is one thing. Yours quite another."

Him annoyed? I buried my ire with a cool smile, saying, "My only wish is to clear up a little matter and prevent Miss Clarke from being unfairly used."

"And my wish is to avoid scandal."

"There has been no inconsistency that you are aware of?"

"On her end, I do not know."

"Any enemies?"

"Besides unofficial detectives poking their noses into business they would be better off staying out of?" Sir Edgar parried, growling the words at me and half rising from his chair. "I tell you, the woman has ideas. Notions and fancies. Harmless, of course, but not worth your time, Mr. Sherlock Holmes."

We sat in silence for a half minute, each measuring the other and determining our next play.

"Mr. Holmes, are you married?" Sir Edgar did not wait for an answer. "I have not bothered to secure for myself a pleasant domesticity. I have made money. That came easy. I'm good at it. Yes, I've made money. But no family. I am alone in this world save for my nephew. It is his lot in life to be social. Pleasant. Romantic, even. So long as he does not dishonour himself or anyone else while he is at it."

"So your family name—"

"Oh, family name be damned. You're not listening, Mr. Holmes! Unlike others of my station, my name is not on buildings. I'm not the type to carve it in stone, you see. Put it on paper, however. A deed. A contract, even one of marriage. Then! A-ha. Then you've something to it. Then it matters. Money. I can make money. I'm good at it."

As he had spoken, Sir Edgar's eyes took on a feverish gleam, and his voice pitched downward until, at the end of his tirade, he had sunk into an almost private conversation with himself. It was an interesting change of tack. His priorities were not unique, of course. And his words did not have the scent of a false lead. More importantly, he was solid on the issue of Mr. Tobias-Henry Price, member of the Oaks Club in London, as being his nephew. His subsequent discourse, strange as it was, had built upon that premise and left me little doubt as to the way things stood with him.

It was, again, looking more and more likely that Miss Clarke had been taken in by an imposter. But why? Miss Clarke was not destitute; however, the money in this equation was wholly on the side of the Price family. And there was the fact that her "Toby" had run off before any game could be played against her.

An image rose up in my mind, a flash of brightness lightning swift, that of a gentleman's walking stick swung carelessly, impudently about so as to catch the golden sunlight and throw it back upon his fellow man. An advertisement in boldness, in devil-may-care. Why that image struck my mind just then, I did not know. But it contrasted oddly with Sir Edgar's parting shot to me.

"My name, Mr. Sherlock Holmes, has meaning and weight. What of yours? Pitted one against the other, say, in a case of libel, which would triumph? Have a care, and good day to you, sir."

A RING OF PROMISE

CHAPTER 4

The inn at Holt proved as comfortable as its first impression had advertised, and I awoke the next morning refreshed if not reinvigorated. My opinion of Sir Edgar had not much changed save for a sharpening of that vague mistrust which haunted this entire case. His threat? Ha. That man would do everything in his power to avoid a suit of the type he had waved over me while we spoke in his parlour. Still, his was now a closed door.

My brain, restless from lack of intellectual sustenance, harried me as I readied myself to meet Miss Clarke. I worried that there was no case here. No real one. I had been engaged in a fool's errand.

And yet . . .

"It remains that there is a man gone missing," I repeated Miss Clarke's words for myself. And that is what mattered to my curiosity. I wanted to discover where Toby had been spirited off to. I desired to know his aims. As usual, the pursuit was very likely its own reward.

I struck off for Saxlingham, making my way on foot. A stretch of mild weather meant for clear and pleasant roads. The walk confirmed my client's statement as to the populace—or lack thereof—in her country. In the three-and-a-half-mile stretch between the two villages I passed only one other individual, a sombre parson who did not meet my gaze.

St. Margaret's Church was my cue to turn my steps northeasterly. The grey-stone with its very squared-off profile looked quite tired, even in the spring sunshine. I passed it by, setting my eyes to the distant gables of Twayside House. Approaching, I saw that the home of Miss Clarke's cousin bore all the marks of a hunting lodge that had been ambitiously expanded upon. Surrounded by an obligatory and proper starched crinoline of trees, the building seemed as guileless as Miss Clarke herself.

Still, I had at least one charge to level at my client, and this I did within moments of our sequestering within Twayside's airy drawing room.

"What news of Toby, Mr. Holmes?" Her bright eyes begged for a fortuitous report.

I raised my eyebrows, saying simply, "You lied to me, Miss Clarke."

An almost invisible tremor passed through the woman's face, but her voice maintained its innocent lilt as she asked, "On what particular was I untruthful?"

"In discussing Tobias-Henry's uncle, you told me that you could not quarrel with a man you had never met. I called on Sir Edgar yesterday afternoon. He considers you quite a fine woman in spite of your impertinent streak and says that you have visited him in his home."

"Oh." The word gushed out of her, and Miss Clarke sank into a chair. She flushed. "I felt I had overstepped with my accosting Mr. Price outside of his club and so felt I should not divulge my other indiscretion. It did not seem to matter at the time of my bringing my troubles to you. My having met him had no bearing on who he believes his nephew to be. Toby's disappearance was, to my mind, unconnected with that prior foolishness on my part."

"You met with Sir Edgar before Mr. Price's disappearance?"

"Before I discovered there was another man publicly using his name and circumstance, yes. Again, as I say, we had made amends. He elicited from me a promise that, soon as my cousin's health permitted, we would marry. We would marry and leave England for the far-flung shores of our youth. Half-promises in letters are one thing, Mr. Holmes. But to have such declarations forwarded in person?" Miss Clarke flushed again. "I could not help but accept, even on the heels of our disagreement. But then—nothing. The fifth of May was the last I saw Toby. We had a picnic lunch.

"It was in hearing nothing from him for weeks after that I became angered, thinking of Sir Edgar's warning me off from Mr. Price in that letter from long ago. And so, on the thirtieth of May, I called upon Toby's uncle, and he merely informed me that his nephew was now in London and that I must be mistaken as to the way things stood between myself and Mr. Price."

"And so you undertook the effrontery of confronting Mr. Tobias-Henry Price in public, thus discovering the strange dupery which sent you to my doorstep."

Miss Clarke lowered her gaze. Her reply was barely audible as she said, "I meant to return his ring to him and found a stranger in his place. It was then that I began to fear that something had happened to my Toby, for what else could explain there being another man living his life?"

"Mr. Price who you met in London—he does not have the scar which you described to me three days back?"

"No, Mr. Holmes. Its absence helped fuel my convictions that I had not imagined the incongruity of it all."

"A memento is easily discarded. A scar, on the other hand . . . Mr. Price's public presence would make for great difficulty in its consistent masking," I mused. "Is there anything at all familiar about the Mr. Price whom you spoke to on St. James's Street? His height? Bearing? An accent?"

"No, not even a feeling." She shuddered. "That man was a complete stranger to me, as I have said. Not an unpleasant one. He was not unkind. He took my blushing apologies and tried to turn them into a charming introduction."

"The sole connection is the name, then. A name which brings with it a monied uncle who has verbally owned to the Mr. Price of London and the

Oaks Club itself, a place where your Mr. Price has claimed membership. Miss Clarke, if I may be so bold, have you the betrothal ring that you meant to return?"

She rose and left the room. A short time later Miss Clarke returned, her eyes dull and her lips pressed tight. She sat, looking away as she held out her hand. "It is here. It is the ring which I gave to Toby when we were but children and that he secured my promise by not two months back."

"Thank you, Miss Clarke," I said, moving towards the open windows so I could better inspect the ring. The design was simple: a band of gold, embellished with a scroll design on either side of a buttercup centrepiece. At the flower's centre, a small sky-blue stone. I called over my shoulder, "There could be no mistaking it?"

"None whatsoever. And before you ask, the only person for whom it holds meaning is me, Mr. Holmes. There would be no cause to make a replica of such a simple little thing as that. The stone is newer. Toby had that done. Something from his worldly travels, a sign that he always thought of me wherever he was." Her bitter laugh sounded of tears, and I turned to return my client's ring to her safekeeping.

"I have only just begun my investigation, Miss Clarke. Have heart," I soothed. In turning 'round, I saw a sudden flash of light flit through the room. It was gone as quick as it had come. A moment later it was back again, a dancing, darting bit of brightness which skittered across the floor before disappearing once more. I turned my attentions back on the row of windows. They opened out onto a garden path, and I craned my neck to espy what angles of viewing they provided on the surrounding country-side. I asked, "Does your Mr. Price ride horses, by chance?"

"It is how he visited me here—first to scold me, then to woo me. The distance from Twayside to his uncle's home is not long, as you well know."

"And do you often have men on horseback watching the house from afar?" I leaned back from the window so that I might point out the object of my attentions without them seeing me.

"Never! Oh, Mr. Holmes!" Miss Clarke exclaimed, rising to her feet and hurrying to the window.

A SOLITARY MAN ON HORSEBACK

CHAPTER 5

"I t's him. Oh, it's him!" Happy relief shone in Miss Clarke's eyes as she spotted the lone rider. Grabbing my arm, she ran from the room, pulling me along as she did so. We stumbled out into the garden only to have the man rein in his horse and ride away an instant later.

My client seemed stunned by the deflation of her sudden hopes, and she swayed and passed an unsteady hand across her brow. I guided her over to a shaded bench where she dutifully sat. Miss Clarke's face had paled considerably, but she waved me off from any offers to fetch someone from inside the house. She kept saying, "But it had to be him, Mr. Holmes. It was Toby, I would swear to it."

I swept my gaze over the now-empty countryside, thinking.

"I'll have the carriage readied. We can set off for Bodham at once." Miss Clarke's voice grew steady, and she continued, "He will be there. It has to be him, Mr. Holmes. He will be at his uncle's. If we leave now—"

"Madam, my powers are not so deep that I can fly to the home of Sir Edgar in the blink of an eye. Even arriving there by the quickest speed, the answer would not change. If the man we saw is your Mr. Price—"

"Oh, but it was!"

"Then he is clearly not completely at liberty to approach, and we must have caution. Sir Edgar is not someone whose word I would put stock in at the present time, and thus his home is not a place I would go running to. He told you his nephew was in London, and mirror signals from a distant hilltop aren't often counted amongst the most common methods of courtship."

"My father taught us." Miss Clarke rose and repeated my inspection of the surrounding wilds. "To send each other messages in the flash of a mirror while we played was something Toby and I were fond of doing as children. I had all but forgotten how it went. But it shows all the more that it must be him."

"Nevertheless, caution, Miss Clarke." I took one more look around, then beckoned that we go back inside. "If it is your Toby, then he is clearly alive and within his own power to a fair extent. It stands to reason then that he will reveal himself when he so chooses or is so able. Now, if I may . . . You and Mr. Price were correspondents, and you stated that he had hinted in his letters that not all of his business pursuits were necessarily correct within the eyes of the law. I wish to satisfy for myself a few little points on that matter."

Miss Clarke blushed and moved to leave the room. I clarified, "I need only a sampling of that which roused your instincts and promise that I will strive to avoid reading anything not directly pertaining to those senses."

Short minutes later, my client had returned, laying out several bundles of letters on the low table in the centre of the room. I sat upon the couch and lost myself to my browsing. Working in reverse order, I did my best to preserve the sanctity of their courtship. Very few of the more personal sentiments were read by me, and those that were did not stick in my mind. I hadn't the space for them.

Miss Clarke was right. Blended in with the amorous declarations, the reminiscences, and descriptions of weather were curious omissions. These were not the letters of a man who dined in London restaurants or occasioned to the theatre. The man behind the pen was not a man of fashion. Yes, he seemed knowledgeable enough of Sir Edgar's home, habits, and humours as to be believably Mr. Price. But he was not a gentleman regularly found at the Oaks Club, St. James's Street, London.

Whatever this Tobias-Henry Price was doing, and whom he was doing it with, never quite made it onto the page. An oblique reference to "placers" surfaced twice under my reading. I made a note on this in my notebook. This alongside the words cheat, scoundrel, Gangs (capitalized in Toby's letters), and gamble had me forming much the same opinion of Mr. Price's business exploits as his fiancée.

It had me newly concerned, concerned that trouble might well be Mr. Price's destined partner in life rather than the steadfast young woman who sat across from me. Presuming it Toby who we had briefly seen just then—something I would later attempt to confirm by methods best left undisclosed to Miss Clarke—the actions seemed a warning.

I finished my inspection of Miss Clarke's letters with a cursory peer through my pocket lens. I then regarded her, saying, "I agree with your impression that Mr. Price may have fallen in with either bad business partners or has past actions which could haunt him. His staying away may be an attempt at protecting you. If we consider, in that light, the strange duplicity of another man using his name and situation in London, it may be that patience on our part will reveal all.

"But I am troubled with the position of this house, its lonely standing. I would recommend that you should take yourself elsewhere for a time. The coast. The coast is healthful. Can your cousin travel?"

"I'm not leaving. Violet is not leaving, Mr. Holmes. And if it was Tobias signalling? If he is at his uncle's house . . . ?"

"Then Sir Edgar is the one concealing him. From you; from me. To find out why would require time and the better hand." Returning to the window, I ducked my head to reconfirm the vantage points. "I say this out of caution for Toby's pursuers rather than suggesting any ill intent from the man himself. The people I suspect as being involved are not the type to blend in. You will be safer somewhere else, somewhere with a greater population, somewhere less easily approached unobserved. At the very least, it would free my mind and attentions. I would rather not spend my energies worrying about the occupants of Twayside while I work this case from the other end. I cannot make you leave, of course, but that is my recommendation."

"And you, Mr. Holmes? You will be returning to London?"

"Yes, but do not look for me at Montague. Further communications for me may be sent care of Ormond Secker at Brown's Hotel in Dover Street. Goodbye, Miss Clarke. And do not despair."

She stood in the doorway and watched me as I made for the spot upon the low rise where we had seen the horseman. In her hand, the gold ring with its turquoise chip stone. She twisted it idly around the tip of her index finger, thoughtful.

I was already worried about the state of the ground before I arrived at my goal. I have stated that the weather was fine. It could have more accurately been termed hot. The thirsty soil was so hard as to make itself inhospitable to taking impressions.

Nevertheless, the signs were present. I dropped to the ground, and a short history unfolded before me: The ride up from the east. The horse's dancing impatience. Deeper divots where the rider had reared, then fled. I followed that line with my eyes, then, in an abundance of caution, dug for my field-lenses.

It stood to reason that, if Mr. Price were watched, so then might I be. But that which left me —left Twayside—exposed to view, also left little in the way of concealment for any who might play the watcher. Returning my attentions to the trampled ground, I considered my next course of action. Technically, I had two choices before me. Though it was hardly a choice at all, really, considering the likelihood that I would lose the trail of my horseman between where I stood and wherever he had ended his ride.

Having a good idea of where Mr. Price's ride would have originated from allowed for this small cheat of inference on my part, and I made for Holt. And from there? The home of Sir Edgar Price. Or the stables, more precisely.

While I had already concurred with Miss Clarke that our mystery rider was her own Tobias-Henry, or at the least, meant to resemble him, the stables on Sir Edgar's estate all but confirmed it. Alas, I could not manage an inspection of the stalls—I had some theories on the tack—but those same shoe prints which I had found a few hundred yards from Miss Clarke's home had both issued forth from the stable gate in the direction of Twayside and returned some time recently.

Inwardly I cursed myself for having set Sir Edgar against me. Still, it cleared my conscience and path. Moving Miss Clarke could force an action by Sir Edgar and the man—his true nephew?—

whom he harboured. Whereas I could now return to London knowing that, if the real Tobias-Henry Price were in Bodham, then he was alive and safely within his own power at present. And if he were not, then the public Mr. Price was yet my best lead.

INTRODUCING MR. ORMOND SECKER

CHAPTER 6

My arrival to London on Friday saw an oscillation between Brown's Hotel and my Montague rooms. To the former I paid a visit with the aim of establishing my other persona with the proprietors and mollifying any concerns that they might have. I had, two years prior, provided some small service to the Fords and so could rely upon their cooperation in my current artifice. The conclusion: Mr. Ormond Secker was most certainly welcome to stay as long as his business demanded it. Oh, and the gentleman already has received correspondence, if I would be so kind as to collect it.

The telegram indicated that Miss Clarke and her cousin had heeded my advice and were heading to Brighton.

And thus to Montague Street I, the soon-to-be Mr. Secker, went. There, back amongst my familiar effects, I could better *métamorphose* into my new role and thus set about meeting the central figure in my case at long last.

Ah, but first a foray into the Museum and confirmation of such facts as would help me in my planned encounter with the London Mr. Price. My application to the Reading Room had been answered.

Picking through the rest of my accumulated correspondence, I sighed. Mr. Lestrade. Again. He would either have to learn, or he would have to wait. Some nonsense from someone-or-other-Vamberry and—I gave a low whistle of surprise—the card of Mr. Langdale Pike. How interesting. Oh, I should very much like to meet with him again. Particularly as I hadn't solid enough footing to manage an introduction to Mr. Price on my own. Unless I were to resort to Miss Clarke's forward tactics, of course. I penned a quick response, pleased with the good fortune of having excellent timing.

An overcast late-afternoon sky witnessed me leaving my rooms. Quick strides took me around the corner and up the steps of the Museum. Though the esteemed institution had never availed itself of my services—that great case was, yet, in my future—there were several present amongst the warders who knew me by sight and reputation. Thus, though in fact I carried within my pocket my pass for admission, mine was a face which could pass unchallenged when gaining entrance into that great house of culture.

Divested of coat and cane, I hunted about the large, domed room for a seat—not an easy task at such a late hour—and then took myself to the perimeter to select the materials by which I might fill my time and satisfy my brain. Not all of my aims were satiated by easy and accessible reference, however, and I was forced to make a request from one of the attendants. Passing him my form, I returned to my seat and amused myself by discerning various details of my fellow bookworms while pretending to read.

The usual crowd was present. Dour academics, lean and hungry from their having arrived at the Room's opening and abstained from a midday meal so as not to lose custody of their favourite desk, ho-hummed over the great questions of humanity. Scrupulous gentlemen made careful comparison of books in the collection with meticulously compiled purchase lists. Young women, bright and bold, flitted about fetching their own books from the room's grand perimeter to return to a sweetheart's side and whisper their fierce excitement. Everywhere the sigh of turning pages and the gentle scratch of steel pens from people copying, tracing, translating, this punctuated by the ever-present motion of attendants' carts weaving between the rows of desks. I thought of Mr. Panizzi, the Keeper of Printed Books and Principal Librarian, and his request for a large, domed Reading Room some thirty years past. Though the dome's architect was said to have drawn inspiration from Rome's Pantheon, I believed a comparison to an ancient straw skep all the more fitting, considering the busy bees at work inside.

I confess to some small impatience as the materials of my hunt were brought to me at the reading room attendant's leisure rather than my own. I caught myself rapping my fingers on my desk before anyone else had cause to note it, and thus the library's other occupants were saved from a percussive recreation of Ries' fingering on a Paganini Caprice which I had enjoyed at St. James's but a couple months prior.

At length, one of the attendants' carts rolled to a stop by my elbow, and I gave an obliging tug on the leathern handle of my desk so as to make the reading table available. By this time I had engrossed myself in one of the reference books I had secured, Denman's 1875 edition of *The Vine and its Fruit*, and so did not spare more than half a glance as the requested materials were left for my use.

Leaving off my rapid scholarship of all things related to the wine trade, I turned my attention to the sources wherein I might affirm the underlying facts of Clarke's story and better establish the parentage for my own false identity.

In so far as I could tell, Miss Clarke's claims were consistent with official record. Confirmed in the service of the 102nd were both Colonel August Clarke and Lieutenant Colonel Henry Price. The latter? Mauled to death by a tiger in 1855. This left a handy loophole into which Mr. Ormond Secker's father could insert himself.

Now all I needed was an introduction.

And a perfecting of my disguise.

. . .

As clients were apt to come calling upon me for any reason and at any time—I had come to expect that the further afield the problem, the more exotic the hour—I could not afford untidiness in my abode. That said, things were becoming such that to stretch my limbs properly was to upset the teakettle and half of a chemistry setup. Take, for example, my indexes, already alluded to as having overrun their cupboards. Add to that my desk with its semi-permanently congested pigeonholes and the various furniture required for the proper hosting of said clients and the living of a modest life in a modern city. Simply put, my profession was outgrowing its offices.

My bedroom with its overstuffed wardrobe containing any number of costume pieces, wigs, and other similar accoutrements might have been confused for an actor's save for the fact that it was also papered over with the many maps and other ephemera of my work that I had tacked up for convenience. I had care enough to keep that door regularly closed but as a human male of twenty-six living alone? Further self-discipline would be Herculean and, to my mind, a waste of energy.

It was within this inner sanctum that I now secluded myself. Mr. Sherlock Holmes went in. Mr. Ormond Secker was to emerge some time later.

To believably become a dock worker, a street musician, an aged dressmaker, or cabman (I had been each of these at one point or another) requires a dual understanding of one's adopted trade and of human nature. A person must be what others expect; specific in style, manner, and in gesture, while also non-memorable. Success, and oftentimes safety, was as reliant upon the active selling of the lie as it was upon blending in.

The persona that I was to adopt in Mr. Price's company could be none of those things. In joining the "crutch and toothpick" crowd, I must be conspicuous and fully fabricated yet authentically so. It meant walking with a different gait, gesturing with my hands and inclining my head in ways unknown to me. Glasses were imperative. The right lenses could suggest a changed bone structure and temperament without the aid of pencils and powders. The rest was up to the styling of hair and clothes. And accent. And a bold disposition. But if Mr. Price could play the dandy in society's spotlight for night after night, so could I!

Turning to leave my lodgings, I felt a strangeness in my chest. Some unnameable vexation pressed upon me, and as I was already fully in my role of Mr. Secker, I lay the emotional charge at his feet. How many had occasioned to consult with me over private and soul-devouring matters? A satisfied case did not necessarily mean a happy ending for many a client. It was the nature of the work and the evil which I doggedly pursued. My Mr. Secker would be strained like the rest. A nervous man, not overly familiar with London and her lurking dangers but subject to her tension atop his own.

Still, some of my trepidation was mine. My neighbours knew me not, and number 59's landlady was one to rarely cross my path—it was a good deal part of the draw of the place for me. (That and its most excellent lighting, care of an expertly placed front window.) With Mr. Holmes gone for who knew how long, the light would be out, the hearth cold, and all correspondence unanswered. I believe that it simply felt odd to close the door on my place, knowing that I had disappeared into thin air.

I shook myself, thoroughly annoyed. I wasn't leaving for the Continent. I wasn't even to stray further than ten miles from my front step. And I had lower and quite possibly more dangerous men amongst my network of informants than they who I was about to pursue myself. But the men behind Tobias-Henry Price's disappearance had my nerves stretched and ready. Particularly as Mr. Ormond Secker was not the type of man to carry upon his person anything in the way of appropriate defence.

NEMESIS

CHAPTER 7

L ate Friday evening paid witness to Mr.
Ormond Secker dining out, attending a
performance at a local theatre, and then
returning to Brown's. As I had wisdom enough not
to count upon the serendipity of encountering Mr.
Price, I chose to employ my time in the service of
my character. I was a gentleman from up near
Spalding, in London for the Season. The party with
whom I was intending to connect had been indefi-
nitely delayed. And from certain knowledge that I
was soon to receive from Mr. Langdale Pike, I
would discover an astounding connection in Mr.
Tobias-Henry Price and so gain introduction.

Throughout my activities of Friday night and
Saturday morning, nobody recognised Holmes of
Montague Street, promising young consulting
detective. I was wholly Mr. Secker in taste and in
manner, in temperament and in habit. I had half a
mind to place myself in the path of someone who

knew me more intimately but restrained the impulse as I hadn't the time nor the disposition to hear advice from Mycroft who, himself, would excel in such matters as complete disguise if he could but manage the physical energy to match his mental.

My hopes were on Saturday's luncheon and the test I should undergo when Mr. Pike arrived at the hotel to meet with Mr. Secker. Scrutiny by this consummate studier of the upper echelon of society, and in daylight, was to tell me whether this scheme would work.

At the appointed hour, I came down and saw that Mr. Pike had just arrived. He looked around, his face wearing a polite expression of bland neutrality even as I was pointed out to him from across the room. We met, shaking hands and giving introductions.

"Ah, Mr. Secker. I wrote to Mr. Sherlock Holmes, and his response was to direct me to you here. Are we to be meeting him at the restaurant, then? I confess to some confusion. I was not aware that he had a business associate and do not believe we have met before?"

"No, nothing like." I flashed a bright smile and gestured that we leave. "Holmes tells me that you had information for him concerning a Mr. Price. That put him in mind of me, who has a desire to meet said gentleman. He—really, that is to say, I— had hopes of you making the introduction if you had no pressing plans."

Mr. Pike took advantage of the noise and colour of the street traffic to make his more pointed objections. He frowned, saying, "I had expected more discretion from the man than to make my communications known to another whom I had neither met nor taken into confidence."

"Alas," I sighed, shrugging. "Then we must fall back to trite talk of violins. How is your Guadagnini, Mr. Pike?"

He stopped in his tracks, an electric shiver convulsing him for one brief moment. On its heels, a flash of frowning disapproval that did not disappear. He peered at me and said, "What is your game, Mr. Hol—?"

"Hold for one moment, Mr. Pike." I leaned towards him, a twinkle in my eye. "You have paid me the greatest of compliments and eased my heart just now. Having fooled you, I believe I can deceive our Mr. Price, who has scandal aplenty to his name after all, if your card for me at Montague is any indication."

He grumbled and took up our pace again. Up Piccadilly to Regent we walked, our conversation safely blanketed by the sounds of the passing traffic.

"Your words the other day had me thinking of various little rumours over the years concerning Mr. Price. Nothing unusual. Nothing ruinous." Pike took out a little book and thumbed through to a page before continuing. "Mounting gambling debts, unfounded. A series of compromising letters, complete fabrication. Ah, underhanded business dealings, the most promising of scandals . . . all easily cleared up."

"Any women?" I raised an eyebrow.

"Two!" He laughed. "One reportedly threw

herself into the sea in Brighton, a shunned and unhappy lover. The second was a secret wife."

"Actresses?"

"Both." He chuckled again and closed his little book. "Nothing sticks to the man. He is clean. Untouchable."

"And the timing?"

"All beginning a little over two years ago." Mr. Pike turned his eyes ahead, his face dark in thought. "On their own, the details are inconsequential. People in his class jockey for position by any means necessary, and so these rumours come and go. I know the patterns well. I know what has teeth and what rings sound. I did not see it, did not think it, until I considered the aim of your questions and why you might be looking into his affairs."

"You have revised your opinion of him, then?" I pressed.

He shook his head. "I think he is exactly what he purports to be. A flashy, monied pretender no different from the rest. What I have come to believe, however, is that Mr. Price has an enemy. Someone hell-bent on taking him down but who has no idea how this class of man works. Who hasn't an inkling of the type of power and protection that his money buys for him."

I considered the fresh-faced and innocent Miss Clarke. Either this unseen adversary had vastly improved their tactics, or Mr. Price's antagonist was none other than the actual and true Tobias-Henry Price, recently seen on horseback near his uncle's home.

We suspended our conversation as we entered

Verrey's and managed the ordering of our meal. Each of us had our thoughts to weigh and neither of us desired to speak in specifics now that we had left the drone of the pavement behind.

At length I had to have my question of him and so asked, "Do you believe he is who he says he is?"

Pike eyed me in such a way as to demonstrate that the irony of my question had been noted. He shrugged. "Of course. And for many reasons. The first being that to even forward that challenge is to attack the entire system. Am I who I say I am, and how is it you know? The gentleman you are asking over, can you attest that his uncle, Sir Edgar, is who he says he is? And, if so, then his word is to be trusted, yes?"

"But the one does not live here," I countered.

"Yet he has not been out of the public eye for so long that our memory of him has grown dim. Ten odd years is an eternity for such a claim to endure and, if a falsehood, stands as much a danger—socially—to the uncle as it does to the nephew."

I believed that the lie went even as deep as Sir Edgar, I countered to myself.

But why? Some defect with his true heir? If so, Sir Edgar might well be to blame for the disappearance of Miss Clarke's Toby. The timing fit, as he would have acted swiftly once he discovered that there was a lady involved who could expose the whole game.

Too, Mr. Price's failed public scandals matched the length of Miss Clarke's courtship with her man, renewed two years ago when he had returned to England from his business abroad. In any event, I would meet this London Price, watch and learn what I could. Barring any progress there, it was to Sir Edgar that I would likely have to return and soon.

"I thank you for your insight, Mr. Pike. I will allow that caution to guide me. To my mind, the schemes of London society are impenetrable and forever putting me ill at ease. I came to town for culture and pleasant diversions, only to find myself enmeshed in flirtations and heresy." I fiddled with my glasses, allowing my character's ever-present smile to dim for the first time since our meeting.

"Ah, my poor Mr. Secker. For culture, you'll want the opera. For entertainment? You'll want the very people you are asking me of. As for a meal, Verrey's is amongst the best." He raised a glass, and we turned our talk to far less dangerous pursuits.

Mr. Pike and I planned to meet at the hotel's entrance again that night. He knew where Mr. Price meant to be—for he had an invitation to the same gathering. My introduction was secure.

The evening air was fine and freeing. We caught a cab to our destination and talked idly of music all the way there. By the time we disembarked, I had three recommendations for upcoming performances, two tips on where I could better improve my dandy regalia, and knew the origin story of the ring on Mr. Pike's pinkie—a story for another time.

The party was large, yet intimate. Even my careful Mr. Secker had no small success at making inroads amongst the men present who counted Mr.

Pike a friend. But no Tobias-Henry Price. I began to fear he would not show.

And then the seas parted and the heavens opened. And, as we are going for gross hyperbole here, the angels sang.

Mr. Tobias-Henry Price was tall and all-over large. A person of supreme confidence, he carried himself well without lapsing into boorishness. He was a pleasing specimen of the idle monied class. This was a man that horses whickered for and dogs flopped down onto the floor by. Charming. Magnetizing. Mesmerizing. But all in a quiet sort of way. Likeable by man, woman, and child. One had the distinct impression that, without trying very hard at all, this man could be successful at whatever he turned his hand to.

That's not to say that his costume followed this rule of fitness and decorum. His habiliment was loud and trending towards outright garishness. But while the styling was cheap, every detail of his clothing cried "expensive!" I concluded that he might well be singlehandedly supporting the livelihood of his overworked tailor. My man was versed —or at least well counselled—in the latest in fashion. He just happened to employ it all wrong. My suspicion was that he was aiming for esoteric while landing, instead, squarely within the opposite. As people so often do.

All in all, it made for a striking picture, and I found myself drawn to him, like so many others before me, an ambitious bee to a dazzling flower.

Noting as I had, the arrival of our evening's objective, Mr. Pike gave me a glance that seemed to read "and now you see." And now I did see, yes. I most definitely saw Mr. Price and his ridiculous silver-toned walking stick, his flamboyance and flash, his monied *entourage*, and wondered at what strange business surrounded him and the other man who claimed the same name.

NOT A MIND FOR DETAILS

CHAPTER 8

From the moment of his arrival, Mr. Price was surrounded by an ever-changing coterie of fashion and frivolity. My Mr. Secker, while flamboyant by my standards, seemed destined to fade into the background. I had underestimated my companion, however. Not long after the requisite time had passed, Mr. Pike excused himself from our little knot of company and made for the other side of the gathering.

"Mr. Price, how ever fortunate that I should find you here tonight . . ." The bright greeting faded amongst the chatter, and I returned to my own trading of witticisms with a group of barristers from up near Hampstead. At length I turned to make eye contact with Pike who inclined his head to me in the subtlest of nods.

I excused myself and approached.

"Allow me to introduce Mr. Ormond Secker."

Price held out a hand. "The pleasure is mine,

Mr. Secker. Mr. Pike tells me you're newly arrived to London and know not a soul save for him."

"In town for the Season, yes. I've people who were to meet me—lovely folk from up near Weybourne—but their travels were delayed, and so Pike here has been helping me amuse myself while I await their joining me."

"Weybourne!" Price positively beamed, and I was glad for having already shaken his hand for the near-violent energy bursting from the man at the word. He seemed almost keen on seizing my hand for another vigorous pumping but refrained. "That is my country. Or near enough. Sir Edgar lives just south of there. How splendid. We're practically cousins, you and I. And then there are our fathers. Pike intimated a connection there as well."

" 'The poor make no new friends.' " I laughed. "Yes. My father knew yours. He and another fellow"—I furrowed my brow in thought, then shook my head—"I cannot think of the name. Served in the 105th same as your father. Had a daughter."

"102nd, old man." Price's smile dimmed in an instant.

"Yes, that was the one!" I snapped my fingers, coolly overlooking the error which Mr. Secker had uttered. "I'm forever forgetting this and that odd fact. No head for details, as my father is fond of telling me. His stories are all I have in the way of a connection to your family. He is a doctor and left India before I was born."

"I myself was not long there," Price offered,

beaming again. "Making any stories which I hold dear second-hand at the least."

I do not know when, precisely, Pike drifted away from our little conversation, but the party itself became a mere backdrop to my fast friendship with Mr. Tobias-Henry Price. We talked at length of various cultural pursuits, plays we had seen, music we had enjoyed. I regaled him with an amusing anecdote of Dr. Secker in India, who in the middle of the night mistook a stick for a deadly snake and proceeded to wake every man around him with his antics in killing the fearsome beast. I placed Colonel Clarke in the position of voice of reason and experience in setting my falsified father aright, thus furthering the value of my connection to Price.

Through it all I watched him. From the mention of Weybourne, to the giving of my purposeful error as to which regiment our fathers had served, to the dropping of the name Clarke at last, I smiled and gestured and played my part but watched my man closely.

I had before me a gentleman of complete confidence and no fear whatsoever of the connections claimed by me. He either suspected nothing or feared nothing. His enthusiasm, infectious. Price was surprised—pleasantly surprised—to be sure, and there had been some brief change in his face when I had included Miss Clarke's father in my amusing tale. But no hesitation. No fear. No sign that there was anything strange or duplicitous involving any of the others touched by Mr. Secker's connections and sudden introduction into Price's life.

My efforts through the tiresome evening were rewarded at last with an invitation to a horse race the following week. I was in. I now could discard this robe and don another for several days. It was time to, myself, look further into the disappearance of the other Tobias-Henry Price.

Somewhere in London between the entrance to a tight, covered passage and its exit into the next street, Mr. Secker disappeared, and a lanky fellow who looked as though he meant mischief sprang up in his wake. I hadn't with me the makings of a complete changeover, but it served as alteration enough for me to dare the back entrance to my lodgings. It was not as though I feared discovery. Rather, I merely required the practice.

I was in my rooms and seated in my old chair with my old clay pipe in hand within moments. There in the cold dark I sat, not even bothering to light a lamp. For I had already made up my mind as to how I should elect to pass the time before meeting my underworld informant. But before I could become someone else yet again, I must first return to myself. Hence, the pipe.

" 'These troublesome disguises which we wear . . .' " I murmured the quotation and closed my eyes. Nighttime sounds settled around me, and I momentarily considered the abandonment of my intended plans for later in favour of a familiar bed and stretch of uninterrupted sloth. The energies of my mind, however, stirred my limbs.

There were some with whom I was to meet who

required brutal honesty of me. But to gain audience I must play the proper role and wear the appropriate garb. Same rules, different party. To play the gaunt thief, I needed sombre blacks and silent shoes, less flash but more daring. An easy enough transformation, I still deigned to light the lamp in my bedroom at last lest I overlook something foolish in my preparations.

And now the hour had struck. I set off for the lair of my unlawful associate by way of Noel Street, exiting my rooms the same way I had come. The sport of it all brought a smile to my face and made for an easy and unaccosted route. Nothing had, of course, changed at Toby's residence. I hadn't expected it to. Loafing about in the shadows for the duration of three very cheap cigarettes, I felt the last of Secker fade. It was safe for me to proceed into the rest of my night's errands.

As the span of years has grown long since these events, I can safely give some details of the person whom I was to meet. A retired garret thief, my man —we'll call him Smith—had been out of the game for over a dozen years, having been arrested, tried, and booked. Rather than endure ten years' penal servitude, he had instead been transported and, upon his return, turned his hand at acting as a chief advisor to a new generation of attic burglars. Our semi-dangerous friendship was built on an uneasy trust and maintained by sheer will—both mine and his. For to back down was to turn oneself over to the mercies and morals of the other side. My kind liked to see justice done; his kind abhorred a loose end.

He tolerated me because he found me fascinating and considered me kindred in method if not in spirit. I was known as one of the more excellent cracksmen around, and I believe that his crew harboured hopes that, one day, they might win me to their side. For me, his information was often good and—this, he himself claimed—distant enough from his own band that it did not stray close to betrayal.

In any event, I was welcome at Smith's lodging house so long as my visits were few and my requests even fewer. Here on the south bank of the river amongst the long tables with their rough and restless men, in a smoky, dim room smelling of sweat, bacon, and coffee, I was received, and two names were passed my way.

I ran my eye over the slip of paper: Thomas Hall. Keppel Gang.

Smith looked at me long and hard before muttering, "May God help you if a word of that is breathed as having come from me or mine, Mr. Holmes."

"Doubtless there are many ways in which one might have accumulated the knowledge written here had I further time or opportunity." I met the threat with stone-faced calm. "The Keppel Gang, for example, are not unknown within certain circles. I happen to be aware of at least two detectives who keep regular eyes upon the enterprise. Once in a while they even manage an arrest. But this Hall. You are certain he is the man I seek?"

"Matches ev'ry particular, right down to that house of his on Noel." Snorting, Smith leaned back. "Hope you weren't needing Mr. Hall for anything, though. Seems he's off and bolted."

My raised eyebrow prompted no further embellishment. Instead, Smith struck out along another line, saying, "If you know the Keppel Gang, then you'll know there's no flies on them. West End robberies via false keys, business burglaries, forgeries, blackmail. Everything. Everything save murder. But Thomas Hall? He comes and he goes. I done wrong to put clothes on my back and food on my table, but your gentleman criminal, he is in it for the fun."

"Gentleman." An odd choice of word. I leapt on it.

"Educated, then. Connected. Seen over in clubland on occasion. Acquaintances with some toff." Smith waved a dismissive hand, continuing quickly, "No, I don't know who or where. His sometimes-mates would only give so much. As I say, he's run off to somewheres, and so they think he's turned on them. About six, seven months back, Hall goes and says he's turning over a new leaf, breaks with his crew. And suddenly, he comes back, looking to his old gang for help. Claimed some trouble after him. With him it was only a matter of time, I would suppose."

Smith ran a hand through his hair and turned his eyes skyward. "You are in this game too long and mistakes happen. Wrong man nabbed; someone is careless or a person talks. And besides . . ."

He turned his eyes back on me and grinned.

"Every man Jack has a weakness: greed. And with him being friends with some swell?"

The silent warning and accompanying question served as a stark reminder of where I was and with what sort of men I had engaged for this reconnaissance. Rising to leave, I thanked Smith for the information.

At the least, I was not looking for a ghost. At the most . . .

I turned back and offered, "You understand that I may not be the only person interested in Thomas Hall. And the men who may be seeking much the same information may be——" I paused, hunting for the words. I couldn't very well say what I suspected. Not with as little credit as that claim would give in this place and certainly not without proof. I substituted, "Men of an unfriendly and ruthless variety. More so than the gang out of Little Keppel Street. If I am right, Mr. Hall's best option in this circumstance might well have been to disappear, and I can only hope that it was under his own power that he did so."

L'HYMNE DU BOULET

CHAPTER 9

Stopping at Brown's the next morning, I collected my correspondence from Miss Clarke. She and her cousin were now settled in Brighton. I dashed off a quick reply before again leaving to see to my other errands.

My combing through my various clippings from the papers yielded no mention of the name "Thomas Hall." Not unexpected, yet gratifying all the same. For it meant that one of the easier avenues by which Toby's pursuers might ascertain his whereabouts remained closed.

For insurance, I spent the next four nights alternately keeping watch over Hall's house on Noel and the residence on Little Keppel that Hall's sometime-gang worked from. The latter appeared, to all intents, constructions, and purposes, a quiet, respectable home, of course. Its unlawful enterprise within was well hid. Yet, a short walk around the corner, some yards off, a barking dog gave regular warning to anyone who dared stray too close. Low fences connected the yards out back, and I could surmise that a similar network of cellars and crawlspaces further facilitated easy communication and escape.

As I say, from the outside there was little to tell. But I soon had for myself the identities of upwards of half a dozen ne'er-do-wells and their respective habits. Square Toes was always last in and first out each day. Pocked Face seemed to keep his complexion via an application of generous afternoon drink. Excellently Trimmed Beard was an early riser, and so on and so forth. By their regularity of routine it seemed as though nothing out of the ordinary was plaguing their operation. Either the business of Thomas Hall was considered concluded and done, or it made little impact upon the goings-on here at the heart of his hidden life.

I returned to Brown's and found that, in leaving the identity of Mr. Secker behind for a few days, I missed a communication from Mr. Price sometime earlier in the week. No matter. His thread I would pick up tomorrow.

Tobias-Henry Price of the Oaks and of—as I had found out through gentle inquiries—Mount Street. Victim or perpetrator of this strange, invisible villainy? Again the question rose in my mind as to whether Miss Clarke could either be mistaken or complicit. Both arguments were swiftly dashed.

For the latter, if true then there was no need to involve me, save to test the soundness of whatever scheme was being played. So far it was nowhere near. The situation was a mess, if a dense one. And

I had the evidence of my own eyes, both at Tway-side and the home of Price's uncle, to satisfy the fallacy of the other.

I scribbled off a quick wire to my client. No update. But with her apparently not being the type to patiently sit and calmly await news, I wanted to assuage any possibility of her stirring further complications through disquietude. I had effectively removed Miss Clarke from the game so as to check my opponent's next move. Either she was a driving force for these events, or she was a mere aggravation.

Add in this Thomas Hall, alias "Toby," alias Mr. Tobias-Henry Price. The connection of the name, and thus the connection to the public Tobias-Henry Price, had to matter. It simply had to. Either as part of the continuing subterfuge or as reason for the initial plot—whatever it may be—having been foiled. And for the trying of this theory, Mr. Secker had to attend a horse racing event with Mr. Price on Thursday.

Thursday morning dawned overcast and windswept. Not a particularly fine day for a steeple-chase. But Mr. Price assured me that the weather would improve once we were clear of the city.

The gentleman was much mistaken, for as the train inched northward, the clouds opened, and a deluge of rain sluiced down the windows of our first-class carriage. With that, even Price's bright spirits were quenched, and neither he nor I found himself in a talkative mood. We settled into our thick silence, each of us coming to the dismal conclusion that our plans were to be spoiled.

Yet, as our progress continued onward to Alexandra Palace, the skies lightened, and glimmers of sunlight burst over the passing scenery. Price looked my way and flashed a smile. He then shrugged, saying, "The trick will be in whether the weather has ruined the turf. It's devilishly slippery after a rain."

He rapped on the steaming glass with the head of his cane, nodding to himself. In drawing my attention, he leaned back in his seat, laying his peculiar aluminium crutch across his knees and caressing the bright object. "Have you ever seen the like, Mr. Secker? No, of course you would not. One of Sir Edgar's. He has quite the collection, but this one is special. One of a kind. Only someone mad as him would have bothered to have such a thing made."

I furrowed my brow with the appropriate level of puzzlement.

Price levelled his gaze at me and, in a tone dark and mysterious, said, "It is my talisman, Mr. Secker. Gentlemen will risk losing entire inheritances at cards over a chance at having it; ladies fling themselves at my feet in a swoon."

"—And it has power over the wind and rain on a late spring morning," I intoned, picking up the game. "By Jove! I knew you had a secret about you, some pact with the powers above. But can it help me pick a horse?"

With that, Price threw back his head and

laughed. "You'll want to pick a jockey more than choose a horse, Secker. You'll see."

We alighted at the station and secured for ourselves the makings of a picnic lunch. Strolling down along one of the paths leading to the Grand Stand, Price's mood faltered for a second time. He had not said anything since leaving the train save to voice light remarks on the definite change in weather and his prediction that the turf had, indeed, been spared. For my part, I merely made myself agreeable and did not force him into any one direction—conversation or otherwise.

Mr. Price now seemed a different person from but an hour before. Intense and brooding rather than sporting. At length he spoke, "The evening that we met. In connection with my father and yours, you mentioned a Colonel Clarke."

"Did I? Well, I suppose I would have, yes." Though I burned with eagerness over this turn of conversation, I kept my tone bright and casual. Squinting in the sunshine, I raised my hand to my brow and peered out across the grounds and towards the racetrack. The crowd was thickening, and so I slowed my steps slightly in hopes that whatever Price's aim was would find voice before close company made free speech difficult.

The abatement of our pace produced no unexpected fruit, however. Swinging his cane, Price seemed to hunt within himself for the words. Not finding what he sought, he frowned and substituted, "Military life. You don't suppose it any more stifling than this?"

Even Mr. Secker could not remain nonchalant, and I stared.

"Ah, of course it would be. Listen to me: woe is me, a poor, silly rich boy." Bending, my companion swiped his stick to decapitate a cluster of pale pink milkmaids growing amongst the grass. "Come on. I don't care one whit if we're in the seats. But I do want to have an eye at the jockeys in the paddock before they take their places."

This was how I discovered that our entertainment for the day would be compliments of Myers' Great Open Air Hippodrome and his lady jockeys. Now, I'll readily confess to having only such interests in horse racing as would pertain to crime—of which the avenues are legion. Mr. Price's idea of fun excited me even less.

However, he had almost allowed himself a blunder. I could feel it humming in his mind still. Under the right level of distraction, perhaps the real question concerning Colonel Clarke would find utterance.

Stamping and snorting in the steamy air, the horses practically danced circles within the paddock to the great admiration of the assembly. Price had, of course, taken himself straight to the fence and turned any number of heads—lady riders included —with his own bold swagger. I followed, a sparrow amongst peacocks, though none seemed to notice.

Price flashed another of his brilliant smiles and cocked his head at me, as though the jockeys and horses were his to divvy up for the cheering on.

I played along. "Red roan. Half-stocking near-foreleg. Snip."

"Terrible choice, old man," he droned, laughing. "As for me, I'm partial to a chestnut——"

A streak of black shot out from the other side of the paddock. Two of the horses shied and another reared as a ferocious snarling broke over our ears. A dog was loose within the paddock. Price was up and over the fence before I could stop him.

"Yah! Get back! Back!" Swinging his cane, Price dealt the dog several blows, separating the cur from the horses and their riders. With one last yelping bark, the dog turned and ran off through the fields. Several men followed, intent that the animal not cause further mischief.

Price, meanwhile, had turned his attentions on the horse—my roan, incidentally—which had spooked. Quieting the animal, he handed the reins to one of the men in Myers' company and, hopping the fence a second time, fixed me a grim look.

"Were it that women, too, were so easily gentled after meeting with a cur," he snarled, eyes darkening. He then blinked, seeming to realize that he had spoken aloud. "Come, Secker. It would appear that the clouds have followed us here regardless."

Angrily, he strode off. In his wake, another line of decapitated flowers.

THE MOUSETRAP

CHAPTER 10

Mr. Price's moody silence dissipated shortly after our leaving of the paddock. I had the impression that, having impulsively crossed a number of lines, he wished to paint himself as as useless and harmless a fellow as ever there was. And as quickly as he could.

A light drizzle had taken up again, forcing us indoors where we happened upon two more of his acquaintances, and I faded into the background under a rapid torrent of discussion on all things fashionable and frivolous.

I felt as if I had been made to fail a test—though it had been Price who had done the failing on my behalf. My backstory, purposefully chosen for its implied proximity to Clarke, had sounded a fault within Price, certainly.

Putting him on guard, rather than on edge, had been my aim. Instead, I had exposed a nerve. I became doubly glad for having stashed Miss Clarke far and away for the time being.

No new invitation followed the strange and, frankly, unsettling events of Alexandra Palace, and Price and I awkwardly parted ways at the station, neither of us bothering with the niceties of saying we would surely see one another sometime or other. And yet . . .

In walking away I had the distinct impression that Price had paused and turned to watch me leave. I could feel the pull of his eyes upon my back, that same nameless need of his. A mood which had begun with the mention of Colonel Clarke's name earlier in the day and culminated in Price's harsh and accidental utterance following the incident with the dog. But Mr. Secker was a bystander to these affairs. He could not very well force an unburdening. And so I strode onward and away, confident that, while our next meeting had gone unpromised and unplanned, Mr. Ormond Secker would be encountering Mr. Tobias-Henry Price again in the coming days.

Said coming days came and went with their usual rapid regularity. I watched Hall's gang and assured myself of their activities once more. I became a frequenter of Noel Street. And I let all correspondence for Mr. Sherlock Holmes go unanswered once I discovered that Montague had become as interesting to the Keppel Gang as their lodgings were to me. Luckily I had more than one refuge upon which to call and so utilized that small advantage to cheat Square Toes of any real progress in his surveillance.

Overall, the situation had not much changed. Miss Clarke's fiancé had been missing for weeks at least, and nobody yet cared save for her, myself, and perhaps a handful of ne'er-do-wells over on Little Keppel. I anticipated a bad end for our missing man, surmised that it had already happened. The other players, though . . . This mystery I must solve, if only to put to rest the question of what had become of Miss Clarke's Toby and why.

And so three days later, by week's end, Mr. Secker was well and ready to spectate a boat race on the Thames with Langdale Pike. With him I could chance an encounter with Tobias-Henry Price who, rumour had it, had also made clear his intent to attend.

As with any event blessed with fine weather during the London Season, the Henley Regatta drew a crowd of many thousands. Once more, my association with Langdale Pike was key in locating Price amongst the boats, launches, and people milling about along the banks. Unfortunately, our long sojourn into the countryside proved to have a vastly unsatisfying limitation: Mr. Price, we found, had secured for himself a smart little rowboat so as to have an advantageous view of the races. He rowed out from shore expertly whilst our informer pointed.

"How disappointing," was Pike's only commentary on this turn of events.

Disappointing did not even begin to describe. For Price was not the sole occupant of his boat.

Artful hat and light floral dress were all that could be spotted of Price's female companion for some time as each craft positioned itself along the route. I witnessed many narrowly-avoided collisions in endeavouring to keep the pair within sight, and I considered in a new light Price's impulsive statement at Alexandra Palace. If nothing else, it did put into perspective Mr. Secker's not having been invited along to this social outing.

At last I had a better view as the boat settled and swung around so that both occupants' faces were discernible through my field-glasses. Distance and the gentle roll of the boat might have rendered my results far from conclusive save for the fact that I knew the woman. Price's female companion was none other than Miss Eudora Frances Clarke!

" 'Brief as woman's love,' " I murmured, putting away my glasses.

"I'm sorry?" Pike turned to me. I waved off my comment as unimportant. We turned our attentions to our picnic lunch.

A rousing cheer was taken up as the first of the contests began. The warm, sunny weather was catching, and newly freed from the burden that I would have to bring Miss Clarke heart-breaking news at some point in my investigation, I lost myself to the thrill of the regatta.

The races began at one o'clock sharp. I cheered on London as a matter of course. It appeared they might manage an upset in the first contest but were foiled. One race hardly ended before another began. Excitement upon excitement; eight backs bending, straining, and sweating as one; the honest strength, the vitality of it all, could not help but buoy the spirits. A fair number of spectators cheered on the German team, a novelty that would, hopefully, bear repetition in future years. I, of course, would not stray so internationally in my applause, though I was equally glad of their presence.

Through it all, I kept my attentions divided. The smooth skimming of the racers across the water, oars gripping and subsequently churning the water ever so slightly, the cries of the spectators . . . and Price and Clarke calmly bobbing in their little craft at the edge of the action. I wondered at it and, again, felt that curious mix of easeful anxiety. The case was developing new edges upon which the intellect might catch.

The crowd roared again. The teams were off like a shot for the first quarter mile of the course before the one boat settled into that steady but quick pace which separates a champion from the disappointed rest. I noted with dispassionate eyes where, here and there, opportunistic idlers liberated this or that small object from unsuspecting and handily distracted victims. But there was no hard crime out here in the wholesome sunshine of a summer's day. For that we would have to look eastward where the press of people carried within it a different timbre.

London.

Even here in the sun and warmth and good cheer, the city's shadow lay across my soul. Its ever-shifting patterns and noisome commerce pulsed in time with the beating of my heart. I have proclaimed both before and since that I have been blessed with the ability to rise above base emotion —love in particular. But that city? I loved her.

And so I cheered for London's team again as they strove, in the Wyfolds, to make up for their earlier defeat. This they did so, and by many lengths, making the contest hardly exciting. I rendered my applause all the same. A second disappointment from London late in the day and we were about at the end of it all with a last race which promised to be less than exciting. Pike and I moved to depart, Price and Clarke having long slipped from sight.

This was no matter, for by evening's end I had returned to Brown's Hotel and found that Mr. Price himself had come calling and issued both apology and invitation in a note for Mr. Secker. Price and several others of his ilk were going out tomorrow evening for dining and diversions, and he would be pleased if I joined their party. I answered in the affirmative and, the next morning, received a communication naming both time and place: we were to rendezvous at Price's home on Mount Street and from there make our way to the Gaiety to take in a matinee. Various revels to follow.

All in all, I believe I would have preferred a tousle with Hall's Keppel Gang.

THE CRUTCH AND TOOTHPICK BRIGADE

CHAPTER 11

There were a half a dozen of us "crutch and toothpick" dandies who met at the Gaiety the following afternoon. All tight trousers and silk-lined Inverness capes, each of Price's other four companions were as indistinguishable from one another by merit of their plumage as they were unable to blend in with the more sombre and modest examples of gentlemen who passed us by. Two—a Mr. Sallow and Mr. Collins—even sported gold toothpicks. But none possessed such a mark of distinction as Mr. Price with his shining crutch-handled aluminium stick.

My bespectacled persona had even managed to brighten his attire for the occasion.

The great Sarah Bernhardt was performing *Frou-Frou*. (Her last day in London, I was told.) And Price's companions seemed to approach the event with a reverence normally due a worship service. I have mentioned Messrs. Sallow and Collins of the golden toothpick already. Mr. Loughty and Mr. Green completed our small affected company. Even Price seemed to have donned a mantle of artifice, not that he had ever taken me into confidence. But the distance was marked. It made my role as Mr. Secker all the easier.

With disdainful sniffs and acerbic stares at the less fanatical devotees around us, we took our places. Again, the veneration from my companions reached cathedral heights and seemed to render the air perfumed with a ritual's incense. For me, I learned what I could of that which had remained unsaid of my companions during our brief introductions. Vacuous canvases all, with the exception of Mr. Loughty who, I believe, was far more interested in myself than Ms. Bernhardt but not for any suspect reasons. That is to say, his attentions for Mr. Secker did not fall under the same flavour of scrutiny that I held for Mr. Price. I found the whole thing flattering, if I am to be wholly honest.

Our next appointment following the play was a leisurely early dinner at the Criterion. From there, the subterranean Criterion itself to take in their evening's performances and, much later on, a rendezvous at the stage door of one of the less reputable theatres. I suffered through it all; smiling when smiling was called for, witty when wit was wanted, and as disaffected as the lot of them until the passing of the hours ate away at our starch, and alcohol unbent us completely.

By the time our company had engaged in the latest of the night's revels, that of billiards, cards, and more drink, I had entrenched myself fully enough amongst my fellows, and etiquette had less-ened enough that I could finally challenge Price on the curious events of the Henley Regatta.

"I say, Price. You were at the boat race this week, were you not?"

"Henley? I never miss it, old man." Mr. Price grinned and leaned forward to take his shot at Collins' ball. We were, perhaps, mere hours until dawn and had changed over to playing pool several beers back, as the game could easily accommodate our company. My Mr. Secker had come close to splitting the pool of winnings two games ago, but I had lost my lives early in this round and so stood to the side, all the poorer for my poor play. Price eyed me and asked, "Were you on the bridge?"

I shook my head. "Picnic with Mr. Pike. He was the one who spotted you rowing off from shore."

"Ah." Price was engaged in seeing how best to sink Green and did not look up. I half-suspected he hadn't entirely attuned and was surprised when, a moment later, he added, "You would have seen that I was not alone in my boat then."

His shot connected, but the ball went wide, missing the pocket, and he laughed. "That's a drink for both you and me, Loughty; you were right. But then, I'm wagering you cannot make your shot either. Turnabout is fair play, after all. And I yet plan on getting very drunk tonight."

Sidling my way, Price confided none too quietly, "Secker! I believe you would be quite interested in the woman with whom I spent my day yesterday. She is a mutual acquaintance, after a fashion."

A tremor shook me, but I kept my face neutral and my voice casual as I asked, "Oh? How so?"

"We spoke of her the night Pike introduced you and I."

I met the statement with a studied puzzled blankness, a silent prompt.

He laughed again. "The colonel's daughter! Miss Clarke is in London."

While I knew that my client had clearly not remained in Brighton—as her communications with me had implied—I still could not take Price's news with complete calm. The surprise in my face was genuine as I said, "Why, that's wonderful! Here for the Season, I take it?"

Price nodded and looked to the table, crying out, "Oh, for God's sake, Green! Just take the shot!"

He turned back to me. "Yes. You'll forgive me, I am sure, for I told her that we had a mutual acquaintance."

"Is she staying with friends? I should very much like to see her."

"Secker. Price. Pay in or stay out this round."

Price gawked and looked to the table. Green smirked and handed him his ball. "Took your last life while you were discussing skirts and pretty faces. Pay up, old man."

Each of us dug for our stakes, and I promised Price a drink. With any luck he would be fool enough or drunk enough by night's end so as to give me information on Clarke's whereabouts that I might caution my wayward client.

· · ·

We stumbled out of the public house, each the worse for wear. I, myself, was not entirely sober, though most of my inebriation was a mere act. Collins fared the worst in our wilted party, and I had fears he might make a nuisance of himself.

Morning was upon us, and here in this district, which I suspected was as low as my companions ever stooped, the inhabitants were stirring to wakefulness. We were deep into the morning's twilight of an overcast day, and after having bade our little company farewell, I confidently strode off into the pre-dawn gloom with Price, his route home being much the same as my own.

Even as a man used to eschewing sleep when circumstances demanded, I was tired. Bone-tired and bleary-eyed. I remarked, "I believe I shall have to come down every year now, even if my Weybourne acquaintances choose not to."

"Particularly if, Secker. Particularly if they don't come down!" Price corrected. A twinkle in his eye, he looped his arm in my own, and our slow stumble homeward progressed.

The street traffic grew stronger before falling off again. And then, in the abatement of passersby and gathering of shadows within one narrow alleyway, it happened. Two men ran at us from out of the darkness of a doorway. One snatched Price's ostentatious cane, while the other took a swing at me. He missed. Or, rather, I ducked. For of the two intoxicated gentlemen the ruffians accosted, this one was nowhere near as impaired as they had bargained.

Knocking the man hard against the wall, I gave chase to the other. I managed him as easily as the first. Leaving the downed man to scramble away—they were nothing save for common thieves—I brought Price's aluminium cane back to him. He leaned groggily against a rail, swearing under his breath.

Noting me, he straightened. "Other one took off that way. But he gave as good as he got. Damned ruffians."

Bending, Price angrily snatched his hat up off the pavement. He eyed me. "Upon my word, you are as solid a chap as I've ever known."

Wordlessly I handed him back his stick. He thanked me and laughed. "I am beginning to think you're the better luck charm than this old thing."

"I have dabbled in boxing, but the sport is not meant for a man of my build and temperament, so I will admit luck had a fair bit of say in what happened just now." I shrugged and smiled back. "Come on, Price. You'll be wanting something for that mark the man put on your cheek."

Wincing, he raised a gloved hand to his face, then nodded. I could tell that he was more rattled than he let on. During the rest of our short walk he had said nothing more save to thank me again for my quick actions. It gave me time to replay the scene in my mind. It had felt like a crime of opportunity and nothing more. But in the end I could not be certain, and this bothered me greatly. I was glad when Price then mentioned that he should very much like me to accompany him to the Handel Festival at the Crystal Palace in two days' time and, further, gifted me with the name of the hotel where Miss Clarke was currently lodging.

DIVERSIONS ENOUGH

CHAPTER 12

I called upon Miss Clarke late that very morning. Best to have that confrontation when all my fire had been used on Price and his friends. At present I had mental energy and little else, and even that was waning. It simply did not do to have a case which might well be occurring in three or more places at once when there was only one of me.

Miss Clarke's presence in town was but another complication in a series of complications. Events and circumstances where people were not who they said they were and did not do what they had promised to do. My annoyance lent vitality to my flagging footsteps, taking me out from under the grey skies that had grown darker and more tempestuous as I walked to Miss Clarke's hotel from mine.

I hadn't long to wait after I sent my card, for I had wired early. Fresh-faced and attired smartly for her London stay, Miss Clarke appeared an unexpectedly suitable match for Mr. Price as she made her way across the room to greet me, her expressive eyes daring me to scold her in public.

I refrained. Rather, I had nothing of the sort in mind. Instead I exchanged a cordial greeting and suggested a restaurant, selected in advance for its excellence of food and sometimes egregious inability to maintain a quiet atmosphere for diners.

Our short walk came punctuated by stilted attempts at small talk. "Miss Clarke, how did you find the Henley races? Had you attended before?"

Her cheeks reddened slightly, and she gave a shy smile. "Mr. Price was so kind as to make the offer. His uncle—that is to say, Sir Edgar—encouraged that we meet."

"Brighton hadn't diversions enough?" I raised my eyebrow to her modest statement. "Ah but then, nothing can quite compare to London in June. Its social events and attractions, its many . . . opportunities."

Smiling, I let her know that all was well, all was forgiven. Miss Clarke was here. There was no undoing that, particularly with her now having spent time in Price's company.

We arrived at Simpson's and were seated.

"Oh, Mr. Holmes, you have my most sincere apologies for my having misled you as to my whereabouts," she began, stopping short at my dismissive wave of a hand.

"No matter. You are here now," I said. "Which serves the same purpose as you being in Brighton. Your cousin, incidentally, is she still well?"

Miss Clarke nodded. "I would never have left

her had she not assured me that I could be, ought to be, here discovering what had happened to my Toby."

"Ah." I sat back, bemused. "You no longer require my assistance on your case."

"Oh, no, Mr. Holmes! I merely thought that I might help. One should always have two strings in their bow, and though I am only moderately familiar with London and haven't the connections that you do——"

"Your greatest assistance to me, Miss Clarke, would be to amuse yourself in your hotel for the time being. That is, if you insist on remaining in London, something that I, myself, would recommend in light of the fact that I cannot trust that you are where you say you are and have taken to using your cousin's generosity of spirit and the ease of telegrams against me."

Miss Clarke's eyes sparked good humour and a clear desire to rebel against the edict, but she wisely said nothing.

I continued, "Your hotel. And please do your best to excuse yourself from Price's next invitation, should it be something that puts you in his power. Say, all alone with him in a boat on the Thames."

Miss Clarke nodded mutely, and I flashed a quick, reassuring smile before adding, "I am looking out for your safety. As well as, quite possibly, Mr. Price's. Your case is . . . well, it is murky, Miss Clarke. And there is only one of me, and I cannot be everywhere at once. There is an element of patience to be had here. From myself as well as you."

"I only meant to help," Miss Clarke's appeal for clemency repeated itself, a forceful, confident earnestness.

I smiled once more and turned our talk to lighter concerns, trusting to her honesty of heart even though Miss Clarke's words rang false as to her personal motives for acting as she had. For I did not think even Miss Clarke yet knew of her fascination with Mr. Tobias-Henry Price. The second of the Messrs. Price, that is.

Mr. Tobias-Henry Price did not seem the worse for wear when we met on Monday for an early lunch at a nice little restaurant not far from the Crystal Palace. He, in fact, seemed inclined to laugh away the incident following our night out, hastily turning to other talk, namely that of the performance we were about to enjoy.

"I've gone twice before. The choral pieces are simply stunning in such a place as that," he said. "Draws amazing crowds. Costa is superb at controlling the great mass of performers and vocalists. And the drums! Wait until you see the drums, Secker."

"It happens every third year, as I understand."

"And not to be missed." He frowned, adding, "Luckily with the grand sound they make, I haven't a need for my glasses. Would you know it, Secker, that villain the other night made off with both my opera glasses and watch?"

"Oh, how irksome," I sympathized. "Thankfully we saved the aluminium crutch."

"Yes," he laughed. "And I have managed not to

be tardy in the intervening day. I'll have to defer to you so that we aren't amongst the boorish late-comers this afternoon."

We finished our meal and made our way to the park and, from there, to our seats within the Crystal Palace itself. A crowd some 21,000 strong settled into hushed silence as, at the stroke of two o'clock, the performance commenced.

George Frideric Handel's *Messiah*. Fifty-three movements in three parts. Price was rapt at my side, and the sheer scale of the thing rendered the audience silent. Brilliant sunshine through the translucent building elevated the event from grand to sublime. Ten minutes in, with the raising of three thousand voices in song, the true power of the undertaking was unleashed. The massive chorus and orchestra, hemmed in by large dividers and thus amplified in their acoustical power, stirred the hearts of every person present. It was but a taste of things to come.

At the conclusion of the first part, I had decided that, yes, I would follow Price's edict and return in three years' time. The choir was, of course, the heart of the performance. The instrumentalists— tasked with the dual difficulties of playing in such a space and with such a sizeable group—could not help but have inconsistencies of tempo and crispness. But the feeling of it was in there and made the whole of it work.

But while many present had a tear called to the corner of their eye or found themselves choked with feeling, Price's transformation was to grow dark and troubled.

"I could do that," he whispered. "Play, I mean."

Glancing sideways at him, I made no verbal response.

"Come on. Third part always bores me to tears." He moved to rise.

Sighing, I followed.

"Stifling in there, was it not, Secker?" Exiting into the gardens, Price gave an exaggerated stretch and shielded his eyes to the bright sunlight. I could still hear the muted notes of the performance as we turned northward onto one of the many paths cutting through the gardens. The tension in Price's frame was growing, some vibrating vexation of spirit.

"You play then, Price?" My question was not meant to dispel his mood, of course, for if I could guide him further into this impulsive baring of his soul which he seemed to return to over and again, then at last I might have my glimmer of light in this otherwise beastly case.

Price grumbled, "Not even a little. But there are teachers aplenty." He brightened and said, "That man over there—see him, Secker? He needs a pupil. Come to the Festival to pick on the pride and ambition of our lot. Our money."

The way in which Price said "money" came as bitter, as despairing, as any of his other mild complaints. Yet his face remained jovial. He looked to me, asking, "What would you recommend for me?"

"For?"

"For work. For what to make of my life."

"Well now, I hardly know—"

"Come, man, we're talking impossibilities here. Where should I go? What should I do?" Price, for all his pretence of absurdity, seemed quite earnest. At the heart of his questions lay some deep desperation born of, perhaps, artifice or guilt.

"Why, whatever you want! You've connections and charisma enough." I laughed. "I'm not sure what you're looking to do. Travel the world? Take up a baton and conduct the next Handel Festival? What, man?"

"Anything! Anything to shake off these golden shackles." He groaned and put a hand to his head. "I am bored. And I am bored of being bored. Of being useless. Of becoming Sir Edgar in a few years' time."

He turned 'round on the path and, walking backwards, regarded the gleaming glass and iron of the Crystal Palace. "I don't make anything. I don't contribute anything, Secker."

"Philanthropy. There's the path for you, then." I steadied him as he turned back around, and arm in arm, we walked amongst the fragrant trees and flowers.

He shook his head. "God knows I am not so generous. I could give it all up, perhaps. But could I give it to someone else?" Price's eyes hardened. "No. No, I could not."

He dismissed the dark mood, smiling again. "And besides, wealth such as ours is so attractive to the ladies. Oh, I say, Secker! I've a box at Covent Garden this coming Saturday. I'm also inviting Miss Clarke, if that is of interest and— Oh, damn. See? See how quickly I need the finer things in life, even though I rail at them so? Opera glasses. I'll need to replace mine that were lost."

"Saturday will be no good for me, I fear. My Weybourne friends are to be in town at long last, and I already made plans for then," I quickly gave excuse. Mr. Secker and Miss Clarke could not yet together be in the company of Mr. Price. I had fooled Pike upon our first meeting, but I wished to not have to do so with my own client, considering the stakes.

Stopping on the path, Price gripped his aluminium staff in both hands, staring unseeing at the ground as he continued his one-sided conversation. "They say 'no man was ever written out of reputation but by himself.' Let me take that pen to paper here and now. You as witness, Secker.

"Villainous ruffians, whoever you are who have made off with my things in the night. I tell you, take them, fair suffering friends! Take them!" Throwing his hands wide, Price flung his cane from him and stood as though transfixed.

"Price, please." This was too much for Mr. Secker and even for me. My companion's troubled mind had burdens that I dared not sound in public. I bent and picked up the discarded cane.

"Yes. Quite so. Neither the time nor the place for such demonstrations. But soon, my man. Soon I shall be free. I shall be honest and clear and beholden to no one." Price's eyes cleared, and he added, "No to Saturday's opera, then. Hmm. I say, Secker! Meet me Wednesday at my club. I've a box at Comique, and they've something playing that I've been positively wild to see."

A BORROWED QUIZZING GLASS

CHAPTER 13

SHOCKING MURDERS NEAR HOLT ran the headline in the Tuesday morning paper. Three sips of coffee had preceded my absorption of this announcement. The rest of the cup was to remain undrunk and unconsidered. I was out the door of my room at Brown's within seconds.

My heart hammered up around my ears as I made for the train that would take me up to Sheringham. The streets flew by in a blur with me barely avoiding unfortunate collisions with passersby as, in my mind's eye, I re-read the words on the page:

SHOCKING MURDERS NEAR HOLT—A horrific series of murders took place yesterday afternoon at the home of Sir Edgar Price. The crime was discovered by a workman who had come to finish recent repairs and found no answer and the front door slightly opened. Entering, he discovered a state of carnage that this paper will refrain from repeating. Of the household and staff, there were none spared. "The horrid sight will haunt me all my days," said the witness when questioned. Police are naming robbery as the likely motive, and there are no leads at present. It is a rare event in such a district, and the shock has left neighbours fervently hoping that it is an isolated affair.

One hasty wire from the station, and I was on a train to the countryside and the house of Price's late uncle. Inwardly I cursed myself soundly for a fool. How could I have allowed this to happen? How had I not foreseen such a tragic development?

"Because you had your eye on the more inter-esting of mysteries, that's how," I growled the chas-tisement to myself. In glaring out the window, I found that I was infinitely thankful for the solitude my ticket had purchased. For a man half-Secker, half-Holmes glared back at me from the glass, and I saw that, in my state of agitation, I had more or less left the hotel as a careless amalgamation of the two. The observation steadied me.

I disembarked at Sheringham and found myself the quickest carriage to Sir Edgar's that could be come by. The driver, stirred as much himself as was everyone by the news of the murders, took the duty of seeing Mr. Sherlock Holmes to the scene with great solemnity and haste. He had no new developments to share, though the gossip thread had grown long and wide by this time. Instead, he took up a hummed, droning sort of tune as we rode. The regular noise of it proved helpful to my questing brain. The distractions of Tobias-Henry Price's wayward existence fell into the background, and hard fact rose up into the fore.

Sir Edgar's home came into view at last. I leaned forward in anticipation.

"Stop off just here, if you please," I gave the command and rose. I was out and on the roadside before we had fully come to a stop. Thanking the man, I shielded my eyes and looked around the lonely country. From the cab pulled 'round the front, it was clear that the county police were still present on scene.

Eyes downturned, I read the road's history as I made my way along to the disturbed home of the late Sir Edgar. From my previous visit to the area, I knew that I could expect some small traffic. It was not what I was looking for, but I made note of the treads of various conveyances nonetheless.

My sense of reason chided me, lest I fall to the glamour of easy suggestion. Nothing was yet ruled out, Sherlock.

Still, my eyes swept the ground for any signs of horse tracks not accompanied by evidence of a wheeled vehicle. To this end, I made my way not directly to Sir Edgar's home but towards the stables.

"Hullo! You there!" A thin, flushed-faced fellow hailed me from the footpath leading out from the home and towards my objective. His steps were shortened by his attempt at hurried dignity. I slowed my own obligingly, smiling at this agitated representative of the local police force.

"Hullo. Mr. Sherlock Holmes." I presented my card.

"Oh." The police inspector squinted at it and, not looking up, held out a hand. "Well, I suppose you're welcome enough then. Hired by Mr. Price, I'll take it? Inspector Jones."

I had returned my attentions to the nearby stables, patting my pockets and finding I hadn't my glass with me. Oh, that damnable Secker! Stepping carefully, I peered into the disturbed dirt and grass leading out from the stable's gate.

"All victims were up in the house, Mr. Holmes," the inspector weathered my distraction with admirable patience before finally venturing to interrupt. Distantly I noted that my attentions had pulled his own ground-ward. But what information he was gathering from his blank stares I couldn't fathom.

Leaning, I grabbed the lintel and peered into the dim of the stables. "Inspector? Could you see that nobody disturbs this area—ground included—until I've returned and given it my full consideration?"

Turning back, I beamed and indicated that he lead onward to the house.

I had not corrected Inspector Jones when he assumed I was there at Mr. Price's behest. It occurred to me, as we entered the darkened home, that Mr. Price could well be present in the aftermath of such a tragedy. Which could potentially make things very awkward.

The fear was unfounded, and only a handful of police from Holt and the surrounding remained on scene, disturbing and running over everything but, of course, they themselves assuming that they were not.

Only Jones seemed to carry within him the sense not to tread carelessly over such thoroughfares as might provide evidence. I suspected he had learned that lesson just a moment ago, outside by the stables.

Pausing in the foyer, I glanced around. Parlour to the left. Stairwell ahead, leading up into darkness. Front door—

I again cursed my lack of magnifying glass.

"Sir Edgar's study?" I inquired. Jones obliged.

"To the side, please," Inspector Jones gave gentle instruction to the two policemen whom we passed on the stairs, indicating with a gesture the more circumspect way in which we had ascended. "Oh, and see to it that nobody goes near the stables. Mr. Holmes wants it untouched."

Ignoring the curious glances which followed his pronouncement, we proceeded. Jones stopped in the hallway, many steps short of the open door at its end. "Fair warning, Mr. Holmes."

We entered the room, and I saw that his caution had been warranted. Though the body of Sir Edgar Price had been taken away for a proper postmortem, the amount of blood present on and around the study desk marked the incredible violence that had been done against the man.

"Found in the chair, there?" I asked.

"Tied to it and beaten almost beyond recognition." Jones pointed. "Ropes there. It was us that cut them, though there isn't anything particular in the knotting, so far I can tell. The rope itself is commonplace. Possibly from the stables."

"The desk?"

The inspector blanched. "We hadn't known you were coming and—"

"May I?" I had leaned far over the desk, hunting with my eyes before pointing.

"By all means," he said.

The object of my attentions? A heavily-ornamented and rather old-fashioned quizzing glass. I liberated it from amongst the scattered papers. Curious little thing. It would have to suffice.

Dropping to the floor, glass between myself and the blood-spattered carpet, I gestured with my free hand that Inspector Jones continue.

He cleared his throat, nervously darting his head to follow my movements as I crept along the ground. He said, "The bodies have been taken away—Sir Edgar and such members of the household who fell to the would-be robbers. The desk here, the filings and safe, those we touched only in an attempt to discover motive."

"And the curtains? Has their position any particular relevance to the crimes which occurred yesterday in this house?"

"They were drawn back last night. One of the men must have shut them."

"Ah. So working in the dark is a personal preference," I quipped, not looking up from my investigations.

Jones hurried across the room to open the curtains.

I rose and fixed my eye upon the policeman. " 'Would-be robbers?' "

He froze, then explained, "If you'll note the state of the filings here, the desk and shelves, and the rooms downstairs . . . It seems to me these men either did not find what they sought or were so incredibly unlucky that they found it in the last place they looked."

"Sir Edgar was beaten. There is always the possibility of revenge," I countered.

"In my experience, it takes a pretty specific brand of revenge to cudgel a butler, maid, and cook in addition to the master of the house."

"Had Sir Edgar a groom?"

"There was no body. We are looking for him now. Managed to keep that detail from the papers at least. Less panic that way."

I looked at Inspector Jones as if really seeing him for the first time. It was a pity that this man operated out of Holt. With a nod, I turned my attentions to the desk and its rifled contents. "Motive. Have you a theory?"

"Sir Edgar's check book has an interesting story to tell, for one." Jones approached. "You'll see that he just yesterday wrote a very large check to his nephew, Mr. Tobias-Henry Price. Not entirely curious, of course, save for the timing of it, the fact that the check itself is still there in the book, and from Sir Edgar having crossed it."

"A rather unusual precaution against fraud for a simple transaction from an uncle to a nephew, yes."

Inspector Jones shrugged. "We've wired to both that establishment as well as Mr. Price's usual bank to see if there's been any recent change we ought to know of."

Ah, a change of bank. How interesting, indeed.

"I've Sir Edgar's bankbook. And his safe contained an orderly—well, once orderly—series of monthly statements. As you can see, yesterday's intended payment is far from ordinary, Mr. Holmes." Inspector Jones crossed his arms and looked me over.

"It may interest you to know that I was with Mr. Price for all of yesterday afternoon." I met the unspoken question with measured calm.

Inspector Jones' flushed aspect renewed itself. "Beg pardon. I have to ask such questions, in light of—"

I waved off the apologies. "Your telegram to each bank may prove informative on the matter. I thank you for directing my attentions onto the check. But seeing as it and the bank records are both present, if thumbed by our assailants, have you formed any ideas as to the true aim of their—as you say, foiled—quest?"

"No, sir."

I grunted and moved onward. Sir Edgar's quizzing glass accompanied us the length and breadth of the house. Inspector Jones pointed out the places where each of the other victims had been found. Stopping at a set of well-appointed rooms as burgled as the rest, the policeman pointed. "That would be Mr. Price's rooms. Not a word from him as of yet, but then you've now told me that he is in London at present."

Jones' theory that the robbery had been unsuccessful grew stronger with each drawer, shelf, nook, and cranny seen overturned or left in disarray. All upholstered chairs had been slashed and rummaged. Mattresses, too. Our bleak tour ended in the home's library, and I was able to see firsthand the collection of walking sticks Mr. Price had once mentioned to me. Picking my way through piles of overturned books that littered the floor, I raised an eyebrow to this last bit of pique from the robbers.

Yes, they had definitely been searching for something particular. The racks of canes had been half-emptied. Heads had been tried; false bottoms sounded. Any which could have concealed some small object had been opened and then tossed to the side.

"And yet . . ." Turning, I made for the front door and, making what observations I could after hours of foot traffic, pictured for myself the multiple scenarios which I yet considered. Following the scent, I returned to Sir Edgar's study, Inspector Jones close on my heels.

That door, too, received the full attention of my borrowed glass. As did the room's mantle and accompanying hearth, corner chair, and—for thoroughness—window sill and surrounding carpet there. I could feel Jones rein in his questions for me as I lastly examined the wall and patch of carpet just to the side of the study door. I stood and, returning to the desk, felt a surging satisfaction shudder through my mind as I gazed upon the disturbed stratum of personal effects that littered its surface.

The last tumbler slid into place, and the lock clicked open in my mind. I looked to Jones. "Consider, if you will: two men who come calling, late yesterday afternoon. One is of medium height, heavy build, enjoys second-rate cigars, uses Maccasarine Oil, and wears square-toed shoes. His associate and, I believe, rather more the lead man of the pair, is of taller stature, thinner build, has slightly more expensive tastes in hats, and exercises more care with his things. They arrive, presenting as business men, both in attire and attitude. Oh, and the latter will more than likely have a beard. Dark and trim.

"Admitted into the house, they meet with Sir Edgar in his study. A business meeting, after a fashion. A discussion ensues, and a large check is requested of Sir Edgar—this through some sort of duress, possibly the threat of blackmail. You'll note the London paper on the desk. It is missing one page, a fact which I shall return to shortly."

While I spoke, I had moved to stand beside the fireplace. "Our bearded villain stood here at one point during the interview, while the other . . ." Long strides took me over to the patch of carpet just inside the doorway. "Here."

"Mr. Holmes—" The policeman moved to make his objections.

I held up a hand, continuing, "The whole interview lasts, perhaps, four minutes. During this time, a second-rate cigar is smoked and various threats and promises are made against Sir Edgar who, in the end, helplessly complies with the extortionous request. Ah! But an unexpected development now comes about. A disturbance in the hall below. Another party, a rival interest, has entered. A complication."

I turned to face the open doorway, gesturing to the corresponding parts of the house. "Butler— taken out with a blow to the head as several men enter at the front door. They then split up, giving the cook and maid the same violent end before beginning their search of the house. It was this second party that bound and beat Sir Edgar. As to our pair of extortionists, I am of a mind that we will likely find two more bodies in the neighbour-hood before long."

"Mr. Holmes! How on earth could you guess at all that!" Inspector Jones stood agog.

I fixed him a withering glare and snorted. "Guess? It's all here, plain and obvious as can be."

"But the timing, the idea that two groups of criminals both struck?" He shook his head. "That's all a bit too far for me."

I bent and pointed to a minute divot in the wall behind me. "Where the door banged open to admit the second party. Having met Sir Edgar myself, I cannot imagine this defect would have happened much earlier than yesterday, for it would not have been allowed to remain for long. Here, the ash from Square Toes' cheap cigar. There, the remainder of the cigar lies in the grate, its owner having been dispatched. Four minutes. Theirs was not a violent entrance, Inspector. You have seen the check and remarked on its singularity; have, too, determined that the frantic housebreakers had a specific goal in mind and that this aim was likely not realized. The state of Sir Edgar's desk, the state of"—I waved about—"everything served as a handy covering up of the first incursion. Save for the newspaper."

"Ah." Inspector Jones smiled.

"One of the London papers. Morning edition. But with a page missing."

With a nod, I invited the inspector to make his brief examination.

"The rifling, the murder, they served to mask the initial party's intents but, in turn, confirm that the paper was whole before Sir Edgar's murder. I can see now how the blood has splashed here and . . . here." His smile widened, and he turned to me, exclaiming, "Great heaven, you're right! But what could it all mean?"

"Motive." With a raised eyebrow, I gave my answering smile. "Come. I've my own theory in need of trying down in the stable."

WHERE SQUARE TOES MET
HIS END

CHAPTER 14

W e headed down and out of the house, and I pointed at two abandoned hats as we passed. Belonging to the first party to arrive at Sir Edgar's the day before, I had given each article a close inspection on my first circuit of the building. I could hear Inspector Jones' faint exclamation of recognition and recollection. I smiled inwardly.

The stables had a fair bit to tell. Sidestepping any tracks as best we could, the inspector and I entered the space to find two horses calmly eyeing us from their respective stalls. But the ground told of four others recently admitted and temporarily tied up within the walkway which connected the stalls to the carriage house. I pointed to the prints, and he nodded.

"Harness room. To see about that rope." He indicated, moving off.

Me, I turned to our brown-eyed, gently-whickering audience of two.

"Oh, the story you could tell us," I murmured. I moved off to follow the policeman into the next room. "Inspector, someone will have to be sent to care for those horses."

"Look here, Mr. Holmes." Jones beckoned. "Peculiar taste in tack, wouldn't you say?"

I felt my face grow grim. Running a gloved hand over the saddle and halter, I frowned. Yes, a thin layer of dust came away from the leather, and not the dust of riding. "This has not been used in some weeks. While not neglected, it has not been duly cared for either."

"Western style, though. And quite expensive. Curious."

"Yes. Come." We made a quick examination of the groom's quarters. I gave a low whistle, finding what I sought. I asked, "Sir Edgar's groom, have we any history for him? Was he, for example, of a military background?"

"I don't believe so, sir. Local man, I think. Not sure he ever even went as far as East Beckham."

"Ah, then." I lifted a small leather pack from a hook on the wall. Out came my little lens as I examined its contents. "Rather unusual possession for him to have, don't you think?"

"A heliograph! Not common, no. Perhaps it had sentimental value."

Thoughtful, I strode off and out into the late-afternoon sunshine.

"And your theory, Mr. Holmes? Has it been satisfied?"

I set my jaw to the conclusions I had just reached and made no response. I now knew who had been playing at being Miss Clarke's "Toby" in recent days. I also had a fairly confirmed idea of where the real Tobias-Henry Price had been while away on his uncle's business two years back, what he had been up to while there, and thus who had set him to running for his life several weeks ago.

Pausing, I asked, "If I could beg one more indulgence of you today, Inspector? I should like to see Sir Edgar."

I kept my thoughts to myself during our quick journey to the morgue. An uneasy humour had taken hold of me, the weight of guilt. Guilt that my involvement in Price's affairs could well have been what had forced the move by his pursuers. I had seen to it that Miss Clarke removed herself from the neighbourhood in hopes of prompting an action. I had repeatedly surveilled the Keppel Gang's base of operation, earning their small interest in me.

But the four riders with their likely connection to Mr. Tobias-Henry Price, aka Thomas Hall . . . They were the true danger, both now and as before, back when I had but an inkling of their existence and intents.

Like the silent occupants of the Price family stables, I had my doubts that Sir Edgar's body should have anything new to tell me. Further, the case would be relying upon the opinions of some country physician of unknown expertise. Still, I had made most of my conclusions at the house.

Our arrival at the mortuary unveiled a new development. A new body had been added to the sad collection within the hour. A bloated, drowned man had been found in Selbrigg Pond, Constable Linsdell explained to us after making brief introductions.

"Was he wearing square-toed shoes?" Inspector Jones fielded the question and was met by stammering confirmation of this fact. Thus Constable Linsdell was surprised by our unsurprise and ushered us in to see Sir Edgar's body as requested.

The battered corpse was in much the condition I anticipated, having seen the scene of his murder —the disarray of implied violence, the scattered blood. Broken fingers. A heavy gash across his nose. Three separate blows to the side and back of his head. Innumerable bruises.

"Here we are, wishing we had a way to definitively tell whether some of this came after death." The constable broke the silence. "But bruises, so far as I am aware, haven't been studied as they ought. Then again, cases like this don't come up often, thank Heaven."

Constable Linsdell shook his head in dismay and went off to leave us on our own.

"Conclusions, Mr. Holmes?" Inspector Jones prompted.

"The other bodies, Inspector." My clipped response escorted the policeman back into disciplined patience.

The rest of the victims, the household staff, had less to tell than even Sir Edgar. Each had succumbed to quick and easy elimination via some blunt instrument. The wounds conjured ideas of some easily concealed, non-remarkable leaded cudgel.

No, the attentions of our criminals had been lavished fully upon Sir Edgar. And from the extent of the injuries, by the methodical cruelty of the minds of they who had carried out such violence, his death had neither been swift nor painless.

"There is revenge in it," I muttered, returning to Sir Edgar's body with my lens. "But the evidence of that frantic search has me believing there was interrogation, too."

I straightened, shouting, "Constable Linsdell?"

He returned to us with all the swiftness of a guilty eavesdropper.

"Yes, Detective?"

"You'll be receiving another body before long, unless our murderous individuals were simply careless in the disposal of but one of the rival gang of criminals."

"Two parties!" Constable Linsdell stared.

"Evidence at the house—and lying here—suggests that, yes."

"Could be a quarrel amongst their own, we don't know—"

"I know! That alone should be sufficient for you." I bit off sharp anger and lapsed back into tense silence as I took one more look at the cold array of death laid out around us.

Half a dozen brutal deaths from a case that had promised to be little more than a curious puzzle. Mr. Tobias-Henry Price had better have heeded my hasty wire. He had damn well better be spending his Tuesday smoking at his club and reading the—

Double damn.

"Have you any of the London papers on hand, Constable?"

I had earned his dislike with my biting response to his well-meant objection. Inspector Jones stepped between us, explaining which paper we needed and why. Grumbling to himself, the constable shuffled through a swaying stack of papers.

"The groom, I believe he will be as difficult to find as the rest of this gang. This was not some crime of impulse. They've been waiting. They have been here for some time." I waved off the question I could see in Jones' face. "Not here, directly. I mean here on English soil. And the murders were personal, yes. I do not believe the others of your district in any danger from these men. They have another goal in mind. One that has not yet been achieved, as you yourself have surmised."

The constable passed the paper my way, and I thanked him, turning back to Inspector Jones. I waved the paper and said, "I will be in touch. Thank you, Inspector, you are a rare gem. I've a detective in town who could use ten like you."

With that, I made my escape towards Twayside House. The itch of worry had been growing in the back of my mind since reading the morning's news, and here it would be answered.

Sadly, the tragedy of Sir Edgar's home was repeated in miniature at Twayside. Here, the door had been forced, but the disarray was the same. Complete even down to the body of the faithful butler. No police had yet been called to this house, for the only witness had been bludgeoned. I had warned the rest of the home's occupants away.

The shadows were growing long, but with an undisturbed scene, I managed a somewhat thorough investigation of the home. It was enough to ascertain that the same men—minus the two Keppel Gang—had entered and searched just as they had Sir Edgar's house. In Twayside the search was cursory, as though even the searchers hadn't quite believed their prize would have been hidden there. Still, from the number of them and the haphazard mess left in their wake, I could not manage any descriptor of the men save that there were four of them, and Sir Edgar's groom was not among their company.

I returned to the train station by way of Holt, stopping off to inform Jones of the latest developments. My input there had reached its end. London called. London and a hasty cataloguing of my chess pieces still on the board. Again I thought of Price and whether he would have heeded my message. Either he had not yet heard the news of Sir Edgar's murder or he had chosen not to come.

It was only when I settled into my carriage on the train that I looked to the paper that Constable Linsdell had found for me. I thumbed through the sheaf, confirming that the only page that had been missing from Sir Edgar's copy had been the one. Taking the one page and leaving the rest had been a foolish error on the part of our murderers. A mistake which I hoped to take full advantage of.

A mistake which now gave me motive, clue, answer . . . all of it.

Mr. Thomas Hall had been arrested several weeks prior on the charge of uttering false coinage. His trial and sentencing but days ago. According to the account of the thing, he had rather cheerfully pleaded guilty.

A TALE OF BALDY MOUNTAIN

CHAPTER 15

I had to get to Thomas Hall first and so wired Newgate from the Norwich station before catching the very last, very late night train into town. Price, fake-Price, whoever he was, could wait. Miss Clarke, she was presumably where I had left her. I had located her Toby at long last, and I was not about to lose him. With his enemies pressing and the man not in any position to defend himself while thinking himself safe within his cell, I needed to get to him before they did. An extra guard, at the least, was warranted. This, and the notice that I was to be posting bail for this same prisoner sometime in the morning, constituted the main points of my quick communiqué.

I returned to London just before dawn and caught a cab to number 59. There I nigh well collapsed. The rest of the world could sleep. Why not I?

The day came, and I hastened to Newgate

where with my being, well, me, rules could be bent and proper proceedings both hushed and sped up. Even with that consideration, however, bureaucratic wheels do not turn fast, and it was fully midday before my aims were satisfied.

Standing at last outside Mr. Hall's cell door, I waited while the prisoner reluctantly shuffled about, complaining. "Tell the man t' leave me be. I done it. I'll do my time."

"Mr. Hall, I am a friend. Sent by Miss Clarke," I spoke loudly and crisply and nodded to the waiting policeman. "I can promise you I have your best interests in mind and have even undertaken consultation on the sad circumstances happening yesterday at the home of Sir Edgar Price."

Hall hurried to the door, watching me all the while. The height, the build, the scar below his right eye, all were as Miss Clarke had described.

"Pleased to make your acquaintance at long last, Mr. Price," I muttered.

The man tensed then relaxed. "I see. Oh, I see. Yes, I will accept liberation at your hands, Mr.—?"

"Holmes. Sherlock Holmes."

He sneered and then sulked alongside. All semblance of bravado evaporated, however, soon as we had left Newgate behind. I watched as Price swivelled his head from side to side as if in anticipation of imminent attack.

"Come. I've somewhere we can talk. Safely. Somewhere your pursuers won't think to look," I said, hailing a four-wheeler. Giving our surroundings the same quick scrutiny that Hall had, I followed my man into the carriage after giving the driver our destination.

We disembarked, neither of us having said another word to each other. Striding to the end of the street, Hall hurrying alongside, I stopped and hailed another cab.

"Here now, what's—?"

"I promised safety, did I not?" I interrupted smoothly.

He grinned. "Lead on, Mr. Holmes."

The next cab left us mere steps from our true destination, one of several modest lodgings that I maintained throughout the city and surrounding. I say modest, but in reality they were more economical than anything else. And, as I had arranged these secret escapes with only myself in mind, lacking most anything in the way of furnishings.

We ascended the narrow stairs, and I let us into the shabby lodgings. Mr. Tobias-Henry Price, alias Thomas Hall, looked around the dim, small room in arch judgment. He did not say it, but I could feel him giving it unkindly comparison to the cell he had only just vacated.

"Have a seat. I have a small bit of business to conduct before you tell me all about who Mr. Thomas Hall is and how his endeavours have conspired to set a very nice young woman into weeks of worry." I busied myself at my sad excuse for a desk—really the only other true bit of furniture in the small room besides the lone chair that Mr. Price now occupied.

'I HAVE HIM. STAY PUT. S.H.' ran the short telegram that I scrawled onto the topmost of my stack of forms. I had a man downstairs in my confidence, and he readily undertook the sending of said message. I returned to Mr. Hall before he had so much as eyed the whole of the floor, walls, and ceiling.

Taking out my cigarette case, I offered one to my guest. He accepted, and we each blew our clouds of smoke into the stale air for several long minutes before Mr. Price shuffled in his seat and asked, "How was it you found me?"

"One of the morning papers had the alias you've used when working with the Keppel Gang. Two of their company, incidentally, met their end at the hands of the men you've been hiding from."

"So you are with the police." Price whitened.

"Consulting detective. My clients are most often those who feel they cannot go to the police."

"Eudora hired you." He slumped. "God bless that woman. I suppose you'll be needing to hear all about it then?"

He waited until my eyes were on him, then continued, "Well, it all started back in '67. I had been ward of my uncle's for a little over five years by that time. Seventeen years of age and I've the kind of life in front of me that I could only have dreamed of when I was younger. Then he pulls me out of it all so as to go into the heart of God-forsaken wildness halfway across the world."

Price spat. "Business, my uncle said. That man knew business, right enough. It was his life, his whole manner of being. And at the expense of everything else. Business. Oh, I'd do his business.

Then I would come right back and finish what I had begun here.

"Mind you, he knew about my friends, my own business. But what's a man to do, I ask you! I was bored and eager. The impatience of youth was on my side. Unshakable, and with the weight of my uncle's fortune should anything go wholly wrong, I had set up my gang in the city. But Sir Edgar wouldn't have it. And so to the Territory I went.

"Had I known, Mr. Holmes! Had I known what awaited me there, I might not have been so reluctant!" Price sank into memory, into silence, and the seconds ticked past. He roused himself, looking me in the eye. "Skies so blue, you believe you're looking straight into Heaven with all her hosts. Mountains so pure, so bold and crisp against those ethereal skies? Makes a man weep to look on it, to feel that wild and changeless strength. The potential. Yes, I thought the New Mexico Territory would be my exile. But no. That dry, high desert, it became my Eden. *El paraíso*. Paradise.

"Well now, out towards Cimmaron, there's one mountain stands shoulders above the rest. Baldy Mountain, so called because its summits are above the tree line. Now, Mr. Lucien Maxwell lived and worked on a massive tract of land on the eastern side of the mountain but had his eye on the western, which he also owned. That's where the gold was.

"You've got to understand, Mr. Holmes, that land is wilds. And the law?" Price shook his head. "Well, a man like you might not have a job there, what with how easily justice is bought and sold or secured through a man's handiness with a gun. But the manner in which the government took hold of the Territory made it likely that Maxwell's claims might not stand. So with gold fever sweeping the valley, he decided to sell. Parcel it off into as many pieces as would profit him and leave the problems to someone else."

"And thus your uncle became an investor in New Mexico mining speculation," I added, gesturing that he continue.

He wagged a finger at me. "Not so fast, Mr. Holmes. They've some particular ways of thinking down in those parts. You and I, my uncle, we can't hold property there. Have to have an intermediary."

"Which meant that your presence there was to act as enforcer of your uncle's dealings."

"Correct." Price grinned. "It was a role I was well-suited for. Or at least my inner Thomas Hall was eager for it. My uncle's money, of course. But forwarded as if from me, Mr. Tobias-Henry Price. We arranged for the purchase of our little tract of land before Maxwell advertised widely to other speculators. I even had my own little band of *desperados* ready to jump at a word from me. Amongst the hundreds, our claim would stand. Now we just needed it to produce.

"Day in and day out, we worked that land along Jacks Creek; men around us going to both rich and ruin . . ." Price's eyes grew hard, and he stared into the middle distance behind me. "Water became as scarce as that gold and copper we so desperately searched for. You can't mine without water, Mr.

Holmes. Can't mine without it. But we were on the creek, and our claim was firm. I held onto the deed myself. Slept with one eye open and a pistol beneath my pillow."

On this second pause, he trailed off into a longer silence, one he dared break only with a whisper. "That hard, lawless, trying, beautiful place . . . It gets under the skin. Stirs the blood. A year into my happy exile, I killed a man. I could look you in the eye and claim it was self-defence. You might even believe me, I suppose. But I killed a man. Because he made me angry."

He shrugged. "Different world out there. My outlaws turned on me—for a drunken brawl ranks lower than the brotherhood purchased of blood and shared danger—and this time the law decided it was on their side. I fled. Southward and into Old Mexico. Their revenge came in the form of a shotgun ambush, but I outrode them all.

"How I made it over the border and into safety, I may never know. I was bleeding, sunburnt, and half dead when someone discovered me and thought it fit to tend to me. But I had escaped. And with the deed to our worthless tract along Baldy's eastern slope. Somehow, even then, I had thought it worth my ruining them as they had me. Somehow, at death's door, I feared my uncle's wrath more than six armed men bent on my destruction."

Price's eyes cleared, and he looked around, startled. "Have you water?"

As I say, it was not the best of my refuges, but I had the basic necessities. I handed him a glass, and he drank it down, parched as though he relived the memory of all those years before. Price wiped his mouth with fingers that trembled. His eyes blazed fury, and he said, "I came home, three years after having been sent by Sir Edgar, to find that my place had been taken. My place! The place of a nephew —blood and family, Mr. Holmes!—filled with some . . . some . . . pretentious, sneering clerk in expensive clothes."

He leapt to his feet, breathing heavily, and I quickly but gently positioned myself for defence. Price noted the precaution and chuckled, a nasty, bitter sound. "Never you mind for your safety, Mr. Holmes. My anger is a half a decade stale."

He swayed and then sat back down, his head in his hands.

"I was not fit to be Tobias-Henry Price, my uncle said. Damn his tight-fisted black heart, I couldn't be me because someone else was. I was dead. Yet here I was." Price sighed and leaned back in his chair. "Here I was. Home at long last, and I could only be Thomas Hall. Thomas Hall with money, however. My uncle saw to it that I did not want. I had enough to keep me from exposing the pretender Price, Sir Edgar's former clerk whose role in my uncle's business had kept him here in England, whereas I had been off to languish on the side of a mountain with men who would kill you soon as look at you."

"You tried to ruin the false Mr. Price. With rumours of various flavours."

He grinned again, wolfish and hungry. "Oh, yes, I did. But money shields a man if you've enough of it. And the public Mr. Price had all the backing of my uncle. As I say, I did not want. But neither did I live as a gentleman. I was allowed to be . . . comfortable. But little more.

"I soon saw my petty actions as foolish, though, for it only gave me the misery of defeat. My failed attacks upon the public Price's status served only to remind me of my place. So I chose to forget him. Later, I tried to befriend him. You will find that Mr. Wyat Wright is one of the most magnetic men in London. Impossible to hate. Easy to love. I grew accustomed to my fate. I mended things between my uncle and I.

"Then I remembered Eudora—her sweet face, those lovely letters from back before my life was ruined. I wrote to her. Perhaps I needed some way to hold on to who I had once been. With her having hired you, I will presume that you know how far our relationship progressed during the two years that followed my initial letter to Miss Clarke?"

"She showed me the ring. Gold with a turquoise stone. Between that, the design of your riding tack in your uncle's stables, and a few other little details, I had a fair idea of where Miss Clarke's Price had been and what troubles might have followed him home."

"My uncle's home. You mentioned some trouble there, Mr. Holmes?" Price's eyes were shrewd, and the familial resemblance to Sir Edgar faded, and the rough man who ran with gunslingers in the wild West shone through all the more.

"Your uncle is dead, Mr. Price. Slain Monday afternoon—by the men whom you have been hiding from, near as I can tell," I gave my impassive report and waited for reaction.

"The Jacks Creek Gang." Price took the news with nary a flicker of emotion. "And Brenton? Acker?"

"Two of the Keppel Gang were murdered as well, caught in the act of blackmailing your uncle over the secret of your double life."

"My stolen life!"

"You uncle is dead, Mr. Price," I repeated, keen that I receive some sort of response on that matter. "The information that your two associates used to threaten Sir Edgar into paying you a very hand-some sum was, incidentally, the same which sent me to Newgate to liberate you. As I said, Mr. Thomas Hall, you had the grave misfortune of having your name appear in the paper two days ago, by merit of your counterfeiting case being heard at last."

Price swore under his breath.

"Information which your enemies now have, yes." Rising, I threw my spent cigarette into the hearth. "Compliments of your uncle's groom who, incidentally, passed himself off as you—albeit at a distance, though whether this was under Sir Edgar's direction or as protection of his own ties to your Jacks Creek Gang, we may never know."

"Save me, Mr. Holmes!" Price threw himself at my feet. Reaching up, he clasped my hands within his own. "I haven't got what it is they want. Oh, save me, I've no way to escape them except through your intervention."

"I have hidden you." I pulled back, leaving the man to grovel on the floor. "At present, I have others to see to. Miss Clarke. The other Mr. Price. I owe him the courtesy of fair warning, you understand."

"Oh, damn Wyat Wright. They'll be on him." Price sat back on his heels. "Once they find me gone, once they know they can't get their hands on that deed by the methods they have already—"

He bit off his words. It was too late. Silently, he stared at me, tense and ready to spring. And then he wilted. "Go. Go on then. I know how caught I am. I know there will be costs. But know that I am willing to do anything for Eudora. She is my future, the only way I can break free of my past."

"In my experience, a woman's love does little in the service of expunging one's sins." With that cold-hearted statement, I left the room, locking it behind me.

FELONIOUS LITTLE PLANS

CHAPTER 16

Brown's hotel again received Mr. Sherlock Holmes and, a short time later, saw Mr. Ormond Secker leave. London still stood within the longest days of the year, and a fading sunlight accompanied me as I made my way over to St. James's Street.

While there was little chance that false-Tobias-Henry Price had barricaded himself at his club on the word of two hasty and dire telegrams—the second I had sent that morning from Liverpool Station—I applied for the man at the Oaks and was turned away disappointed. At Price's Mount Street lodgings my experience repeated itself, only now I was trying the patience of the butler.

"Mr. Price has gone to the theatre and will be gone for the rest of the evening, Mr. Secker."

"Yes, yes," an exasperated Mr. Secker gave response. "But which theatre? I was to have met him at his club earlier and missed my engagement with the gentleman. I meant to attend this same performance with him. Did he, by chance, leave me my ticket?"

The imperturbable servant pursed his lips. No doubt he was used to this or that of Price's friends dashing about. I should know, having met with a handful of them in this very house but days before. Even then, not all had been punctual, and Price had planned our timing with that in mind.

"No, sir, he will be in his box at the Opera Comique."

"Ah! That was the name, yes. Terrible memory for these things, you know. Price has had me all in a whirl these past weeks. This theatre, that restaurant . . . I've become all turned 'round from it." I made a show of taking out my watch and peering at it, utterly dismayed. "And it seems I am destined to miss the performance after all."

With that, I strode off into the night, my bespectacled persona fretting and wagging his head. Around the next corner, I hailed a cab but not without first giving my own name to a policeman and suggesting that he give special attention to the house at number 225 as a precaution against potential mischief tonight. Breathing easier for having given some semblance of protection to Price's staff —well, Wyat Wright's I should say, for in having the gentleman's true name at last, I had better start using it—I set off for the Opera Comique, surprised that he should have attended, given the circumstances. Still, it made my next task an easy one. I should be grateful.

With such fine weather, the pedestrian and

vehicular traffic on this late Wednesday evening remained thick. We crawled along, our snail's pace rendering the ride smooth if slow. At each intersection, a tricky impasse for the cabbie. I shifted about in my seat, maddened by my impatience to return to the real Tobias-Henry Price and reassure myself of his continued safety. But first I must collect Wyat Wright who, too, could be in danger and who I suspected carried the precious deed upon his very person. Distantly I distracted myself by wondering what it was that was playing tonight, the thing Price had been so "positively wild" to see. No matter. Neither he nor I should be seeing the whole of it.

I gave my name at the theatre's entrance and asked after Price, emphasizing that I had been engaged by the family in the investigation of Sir Edgar's murder. Under this, the unspoken implication that my matter could not wait, I was shown to Price's box.

I entered and took the vacant seat beside Wright. He shifted, surprised, and darted me a glance. He whispered, "Secker! Oh, how glad I am to see you! Waited as long as I could at Oaks. What kept you, old man? You've missed the first act and half of the second!"

"You should not have come here." I kept my voice low. "Really, Price! The danger—"

"A-ha!" Wright's hissed exclamation came coloured by triumph. "I knew you were in league with him, with that meddler Mr. Sherlock Holmes."

I blinked, utterly bereft of words as I choked down a laugh. From the corner of my eye, I could see a chorus of some half a dozen policemen dancing about on the stage, lamenting their lot in life:

"*His capacity for innocent enjoyment,*
"*Is just as great as any honest man's.*"

Wright seemed to take my silence as confirmation of the fact and moved to explain, "Sir Edgar had said something of the name, you see. Put me on guard should the man come around. Then—then!—something actually happens, and here he is, poking his long nose in, asking his questions, sending urgent, threatening telegrams."

"Threatening?"

"*When constabulary duty's to be done.*
"*Ah, take one consideration with another . . .*"

"Well, not as such, no," Mr. Wright muttered. "But there was warning in the tone."

"I should say, old man. Considering what the papers had to tell of it, you would do well to take precautions. 'Twould be the sensible thing, you know." I held on to the last of Mr. Secker, insistent I have the upper hand and Wright's trust once more before unmasking myself and risking total dismissal. There was a performance going on right under our noses, after all. It would not do to make a scene.

"*Oh—!*

"*When constabulary duty's to be done, to be done,*
"*A policeman's lot is not a happy one, happy one.*"

"Sensible, yes," Wright mused, then shook his head. "Apologies, Secker. I've been all on edge since my uncle put me on guard over this man. Days before we met, I had encountered Miss Clarke. This before I knew it to be her, of course. But it made our meeting seem oddly fortuitous, for my uncle thought it prudent that I make amends with her as best I could once this Holmes came lurking around, asking questions about her. I had initially hoped I could employ you as my excuse to make the introduction until I learned you knew less than I."

Sighing, I handed over my card, straightening in my chair and letting go of the pleasant and sociable Mr. Secker at long last. For my companion's voice had tripped on his first claim of Sir Edgar as his uncle. It had utterly failed on the second.

"When the enterprising burglar's not a-burgling,
"When the cut-throat isn't occupied in crime,
"He loves to hear the little brook a-gurgling,
"And listen to the merry village chime."

"I— I—!" Sputtering, Mr. Wright almost forgot to keep his voice down, and he half rose from his seat.

"I am pleased to make your formal acquaintance at last, Mr. Wright," I said, unable to keep the warmth from my tone. I, too, stood and moved to ensure he did not bolt for the exit. "Now, I've a little matter to clear up with a certain Tobias-Henry Price, and I believe that your favourite walking stick will serve to preserve both his safety and yours."

"My—? But—!" His eyes bulged, and child-like, Wright clutched the cane to his chest. He wheezed at last, "And Miss Clarke?"

I nodded to the audience fanned out below us. "She knows, having hired me after discovering, outside the Oaks Club, a stranger in place of a friend. But I haven't a desire to expose this plot to any larger circle than ourselves. The larger truth will be yours to own to as you see fit."

"Oh—!

"When constabulary duty's to be done, to be done,

"A policeman's lot is not a happy one, happy one."

The orchestra's cheery closure of the policeman's ditty followed us out of Price's box, Wright shaking his head all the while and stumbling as if in a daze. "I haven't done a thing wrong. You'll see. Not a thing."

"Nothing criminal, no," I agreed. "But not altogether correct, either. Even with Sir Edgar's blessing on the whole of it."

Together we rode to the semi-secret lodgings where I had hid Tobias-Henry Price. Our going was faster as more and more people made it to their destinations for the evening and stayed. But the route was longer from the Comique to my little refuge, and so I took advantage of the time before Thomas Hall would be privy to our words and asked of Mr. Wright, "Did you know where the real Mr. Tobias-Henry Price had hid himself and from whom he ran?"

"No," came his calm, if defiant, response. "On both counts, no. What that man did with himself when not in my company was of no concern of mine."

"In spite of the danger that his existence posed to you?" I raised my eyebrows.

He laughed, a sharp bitter sound quite unlike his typical free and easy mirth. "Sir Edgar and I had no fear of the scoundrel. Price—yes, the real Price—had money enough. And he was never unwelcome at his uncle's home. Spent half his time there and the other half at some place in town here."

"Noel Street," I made my soft remark, jarred by the callous, nervous energy in the cab. I've known many a dangerous man. He did not feel dangerous. But he did feel desperate. Desperate like some masterless dog or an army that had lost its general on the field of battle. He needed direction but had nowhere to turn. And so to me he looked.

Wright locked his gaze to mine. "Please, Mr. Holmes. Believe me. Believe in me. Know that I never meant any harm to anyone by this deception. Every bit of trickery in this, any low thing, it comes from Mr. Tobias-Henry Price. Sir Edgar—"

He stopped, swallowed hard, and began again, his eyes trained out the window of the cab. "Sir Edgar had my full and complete trust. And I his. All the way back to when I was but a lowly clerk for, first, a few of his business dealings and then later a fair bit more. I set him straight where he might be tempted to go crooked. My competence made safe his investments and allowed that volatile man a moment's peace.

"And then one day a social invitation came for Mr. Price, an event that Sir Edgar could not bear to have no hand in, no presence within. But Tobias-Henry was in America—a fact that, happily, next to nobody knew. Sir Edgar proposed a wild idea. That shrewd mind of his put forth the plan that I present myself as Mr. Tobias-Henry Price. Just the once, you understand. Set things into motion on a level that business can only barely reach but that society often can. I was then to melt away into oblivion, Sir Edgar's invisible manager of business once more."

"But the temptation to stay Mr. Price was too great," I countered.

"Yes and no." Wyat Wright shook his head. "It was a slower sinking into captivity, Mr. Holmes. I did exactly as I have said. I paraded about as Mr. Price for one day. One glorious day. Then I returned to Sir Edgar, became myself once more, and gave up the marvellous aluminium crutch.

"The next week, another social invitation came for Mr. Price, consequence of my having seen and been seen. Sir Edgar answered it in the affirmative, believing it essential that nobody know of our deceit. Cornered, I repeated the lie. A month later, I did so again. I was never Price for long. The stories that kept him from appearing for any real stretch of time became harder to maintain. But I—that is, Mr. Price—was becoming known to more and more people.

"Within a half a year, that one appearance developed into a residence in London, membership at the Oaks, and a host of powerful friends and acquaintances who all believed me to be Sir Edgar's nephew and heir. I did not know how to put a stop to it, Mr. Holmes! Not without ruining Sir Edgar; ruining my own prospects.

"I made plans to give it all up. Even if I must remove myself to parts unknown and pursue a new position with no word to recommend me. I would tell him tomorrow. I would tell him next week. And then the news came to us that the real Tobias-Henry Price had been killed over in America. My timing was poor. Here, a man is poised to mourn his only heir, his sole bit of family on this earth . . ."

"So you said nothing."

"I said nothing. I became the nephew he had lost. I was already more than most of the way there, as it was." Wyat Wright hung his head. "By the time the real Tobias-Henry Price returned home some two years later, it was too late for any of us to make the change. The false Tobias-Henry Price was too connected, too known."

"And you had become exactly the nephew that Sir Edgar had wanted."

"Exactly, Mr. Holmes. In every particular save for blood itself." Mr. Wright sighed. "At first, Price was livid. But he hadn't the strength to fight us. The story of his apparent death had not been all that far from the truth. He bore frightful wounds—both physical and spiritual—and so gave himself over to the lies we had made in his absence."

I waited until it seemed that Mr. Wright would not add more to his story and then spoke, "The men who gave Mr. Price those scars have followed him here. It is they who murdered Sir Edgar, Sir Edgar's servants, and the butler at the house of Miss Clarke's cousin in an attempt at regaining an item which he took when he ran from their vigilante justice all those five years back."

"Miss Clarke!"

"She is safe," I added quickly. "Having foreseen some of the dangers posed to her in her relationship to Mr. Price, I warned her and her cousin off from Twayside House before the terrible events of earlier this week."

Something twisted in Wright's face, a strange, poorly-mastered anguish that he tried to hide. "I may not be a true gentleman, Mr. Holmes. I may have the clothes, the house, the money, and but lack the breeding of it. But you can say, to my face, the words and know that I can bear them. She hired you to find the truth of it, did she not?"

"She consulted me to discover where her Tobias-Henry had gone and why."

Wright put his head in his hands and groaned.

"Now what remains is for me to find a way to appease the relentless men who are pursuing Mr. Price," I spoke over Wright's agony of heart and fixed my eyes on the cane in his hands.

"Take it." He thrust it at me. "And may you never have a whit of luck by it. With your words just now, you've taken from me the only chance at happiness I might have had from this misadventure."

"Oh, come now." A quaver struck me, and I hadn't time or brain power enough to waste on consoling miserable Wyat Wright. I took the cane, twisted its silver handle, and heard/felt the satisfying click of a catch opening. I turned it on end and gave it a shake.

Nothing happened.

I rapped the side, shaking it more violently, and inclining my ear to its luminous length.

Still nothing.

I was not fool enough to peer inside and so addressed Mr. Wright anew, "Where is it?"

He met my gaze with bleak, calm resignation, his eyes as dark, as hollow as the cane which I held in my hands. He said, "Whatever was in Sir Edgar's famed aluminium crutch, Mr. Holmes, is long gone. The one you're holding is a clever replica. Made some seven months ago after an incident in which the original was lost."

ABDUCTION!

CHAPTER 17

I gawked. I almost laughed and, in fact, would
have but for the fact that a man's life might
hang in the balance of this unexpected disas-
ter. Eyes on the two pieces of crutch-handled stick
in my hands, I said, "Explain yourself."

Wright's voice came out small as he said, "It was
sometime late last year. I was coming back into the
city from a visit with Sir Edgar. The weather had
turned cold and damp in the miles between Sheringham and Liverpool Station. The fog was thick
and oily, the air wet and positively chloroforming. A
proper London welcome.

"I disembarked from the train and was jostled
on the platform. Nothing serious, just the accidental
collision one is bound to have when a man can't see
his hand in front of his face. I lost my hat and
dropped the cane, Mr. Holmes. And that's where
instinct crept in. Here I was, standing an easy target
for mischief at the edge of the track. The hat? The

cane? Easily replaced. And so I hailed a cab—not an easy find on a night like that, of course, but money will buy most anything—and returned home, thinking little more on the incident."

He shrugged. "The loss of the hat irked me most. I had just purchased it. Sir Edgar's stick, though? It was just an old oddity. A relic of his pride. Even the metal used to make it, once extravagant, had fallen out of fashion.

"As I say, I had another made. You recall my saying that Sir Edgar was something of a collector, yes? I couldn't very well admit to my clumsiness. And thus I've gone about with this replacement with nobody the wiser. I hadn't a thought there might be something valuable hidden inside."

The cab jolted to a stop, and I beckoned. "Come then. We may have no choice but to own to our failures and face these discomfiting truths." I continued to speak as we climbed the stairs to my room, "The police may have to be employed, you understand, now that we haven't a way to appease the men from Jacks Creek who—"

I opened the door to an empty room which had been thrown into disarray. We hurried in and found that the chair which Mr. Tobias-Henry Price had occupied had been overturned. My desk was shoved crookedly against the wall, and some of its contents spilled onto the floor. The glass that my guest had used: smashed at the foot of the fireplace grate. The open window ushered in the light warmth of the summer nighttime air. Its glass had been broken.

I swore and moved to light the sole lamp in the room, glad that it had been spared.

"He's been taken!"

"So it would appear, yes." I thumbed my chin thoughtfully and then moved to inspect the door frame. "Oh, and if you could please refrain from touching anything, Mr. Wright." This last came as, from the corner of my eye, I saw my companion bend to right the chair.

The nervous energy in the man was back, and he bled it out by pacing in the corner—not an easy task in so small a room. Wright exclaimed, "I have doomed us all through my carelessness! How could I have been so negligent? Would they take money? How much would they want of us? And even then . . . ?"

I hissed my annoyance at Wright's fretting, and he quieted. Crossing his arms, he stood to the side and watched as I crept along the floorboards with Sir Edgar's quizzing glass, stopping at the fireplace to run my hands along the mantle, lightly brushing the wall with my fingers, and then doubling back. "Hmm." I frowned, picking at a snag of cloth caught in a splinter of the mantle's rough edge. I moved on to the window sill.

Impatient, Wright clattered about behind me, upending the chair at last to defiantly take a seat. I heard him gasp and turned.

" 'We have him. Stay put, Sherlock Holmes,' " Wright read from the small slip of paper in his hand. "See? They have taken him. Absolute proof."

Frowning, I accepted the scrap and applied my glass. "Strange. That is—almost to the word—the selfsame message I wired to Miss Clarke not two hours ago. Which suggests to me that—"

"Good Lord!" he cried. "Miss Clarke!"

Rising, Wright tried to run past me.

I blocked his way. "Wait! It may be Price himself who—!"

Wyat Wright caught me a blow on the jaw and dashed off down the stairs and out into the night. Dizzily, I followed. A match for me in build and power, his had been an unexpected jab but not altogether expert. Sprinting behind him, I ran down the now-quiet street, fumbling for the police whistle that, of course, Mr. Secker would never deign to carry upon his person.

Wright rounded the corner ahead of me, and an instant later, I heard an aborted cry and a thump.

AMBUSH!

CHAPTER 18

I skidded to a halt and found a pair of men standing in the dark deserted street ahead. Wyat Wright was nowhere to be seen. Stepping into shadows, I considered my options and, turning, found my path blocked from behind. Two others, each stocky and solidly-built men, grinned coarse acknowledgement back at me.

There we stood, learning what we might in those brief, tense moments as the boldest of the gang—presumably their leader—caught my gaze and gave a nod to his fellows. The man at his side took up his position at the mouth of the lane while one of the pair at my back took up his post in the opposite direction. Lookouts both, lest our little altercation meet with unexpected interference. The last, the largest, crossed his arms, remaining close by. Insurance. My opponent's "closer" should he be needed.

"Easy pickings tonight. Any more out there like

you or your friend?" One of the men gave a low chortle. Looking at me, leering at me, they seemed pretty certain that the services of their thug would not be required save for, perhaps, in helping dump my limp body somewhere foul at the conclusion of our tête-à-tête.

Ah, gentlemen, I thought. Prepare yourselves for a surprise.

Combatant one, my thick and boorish friend, dropped into a swinging crouch. Loose knees, his cane swinging back and forth in his hands, he looked for all the world like some mesmerizing, viperous serpent. They were the practiced motions of a professional ruffian.

Thank you for telling me this before engaging, I mused. I raised my gloved hands. My own cane dangled from my fingers as I craned my head in search of the local policeman. Surrender. Please don't hurt me, good sirs.

A sudden shifting of feet from my man. He lunged sideways and forward. His cane whipped crossways at my face, and I dodged. Another swing. Another dodge.

I had not yet brought my cane up, and my steps backward were faltering and inexact. I was a gentleman on his heels, and the lookout to the south abandoned his post to come upon me from behind. Now my cane did come into play. Whipping around, I made a wide, ungainly circle with it and ensured for myself a gap between myself and my oppressors.

"Naow, Mr. Holmes," my combatant sneered.

"Yew can lay off th' pretending. We know yer reputation."

American. That was one point on which I had been correct, then. I raised my eyebrows. "This would be why you number four at the least?"

"Lookee 'ere. The sneak can count!"

"Yeah. And he'll need to. When he's picking his teeth up from the pavement!" The man at my back lunged.

Dropping to one knee, I tucked my cane under my opposite arm and thrust its heavy head backwards. The blow buried itself in my opponent's abdomen, and he staggered on his heels, winded. Turning swiftly, my second stroke landed itself on the man's neck. He dropped like a stone.

My sudden attack brought the other lookout running. Their leader still danced about on his toes, his weapon an uncomfortable blur which whistled close but harmless past my ears. My own cane windmilled between us, forcing distance.

Crack. Crack. The battle joined. Three against one.

Our canes dashed together in harsh discordance. The circle of our combat gently turned, they the hands—date, hour, minute—and I the centre gear around which all movement concentrated. And time was, indeed, the thing upon which I was primarily reliant at the moment. A quick thrust from me dispatched another of my attackers. He fell to the ground gurgling, his hands clutching his throat. His partner, the erstwhile safeguard, landed heavily after a blow to his kneecap resulted in a telling crunch.

A glancing blow from the lead attacker set my forearm to tingling. I wondered how long my impractical weapon would hold up against what was essentially a heavy cudgel. They had come prepared. I had not. They had come at me armed. I was . . . well, name and reputation aside, I was a dandy through and through at present. Bothersome gloves, absurdly delicate cane, and all. Quite simply, it was cunning versus clout, and one does not easily think their way out of such peril.

My last man and I completed our narrow revolution of footwork. Indulging in a half-step retreat, I bent and seized the weapon of the man I had taken out first.

"Wyat Wright," breathing hard, I threw my accusation at the gang's leader.

He smiled, shrugging. "Never heard of him."

Reversing my momentum, I lashed out with the head of my crutch, catching my opponent on the wrist. With a twist, I had his hand bent at an unfavourable angle. He hissed in pain but had presence of mind to follow the motion and save his bones from any real punishment. His stick dropped into his other hand and a swipe of it forced me backwards. My cane clattered to the street, and I was doubly grateful for having armed myself with something sturdier.

"Yer quick on yer feet, to be sure." My opponent's eyes glittered and he issued invitation, hands thrown wide. "Better than the other one. The useless gentleman. But does the Yard's dog bite?"

Three energetic jabs followed the taunt, and I was forced to give ground. Another flurry of strikes brought him within arms' length, and he managed to get a hold of my weapon. I returned the favour, and we grappled silently in our dark alleyway for a brief eternity.

"Don't matter what we've done with him, see? You'll both be corpses before the night is out." The man breathed his foul threat mere inches from my face. He grinned, revealing a line of uneven teeth, two capped in gold. With a quiet *snick* his cane loosed its malevolent secret. Like fire in my hand, like the stinging of a thousand vengeful wasps, cunningly-hidden blades within my attacker's cane tore at my fingers.

I cried aloud—both in surprise and pain—and so had little defence for the cutting blows that now rained down upon my arms, shoulders, and back. In the space of a breath, my victory had become bloodied defeat. Falling into darkness, I distantly noted that several other figures had crowded 'round, heaping further abuse which I, blessedly, could no longer feel.

MR. TOBIAS-HENRY PRICE

CHAPTER 19

Consciousness returned to me in careful spurts. The world was humming to me, a deep throbbing drone which infected even my bones. I shifted, and the fire of my various wounds declared themselves to my attention, an agony which I did my best to ignore. For I lay in darkness, bound hand and foot. Shifting again, I tried the cords. Whoever had tied them was a fair expert.

Inwardly I swore and, again, tried to think around the blazing pain of the lacerations which ran the length of my right arm and part of my left, tortured both hands, and had been liberally given to my shoulders and upper back. Wincing, I was assured that my face and head were but bruised. The foggy sensation refused to dissipate, but little by little, my dim surroundings revealed themselves to me.

I was on a boat. In the aft cabin of a forty-foot

steam launch, to be precise. It was the engine's resonance I had first sensed upon waking. Hissing in pain, I craned my neck to espy through the open cabin door a man at the wheel, his outline dim but visible against the light from the boat's forward saloon. Other shadows moved, and a smattering of harsh, accented speech drifted back to my ears from that front cabin. It was my American friend. The one possessing the wicked cane and zero scruples.

Attuning, I listened for any signs that might indicate our position. All was silent save for the chug of the engine, the gentle whisper of the waves against the iron hull, and the occasional chatter of the men up front. Once in a while, the boat would appear to bounce as a wave struck it at an odd angle.

Not the Thames then. We were out to sea. I considered my options and found myself stunned by how few I had. My first priority was the bonds around my ankles and wrists. But with no back door on the cabin wherein I had been deposited, I would have to confront the man at the wheel before I tried to escape over the side of the boat. This while injured as I was. From there, a swim of unknown distance through a frigid sea. My only consolation there was that I believed the waters to be reasonably calm tonight, if the launch's motion were an accurate indication of conditions.

And if I could not escape?

My thoughts danced along the cliff's edge of despair. Would anyone come looking? When I did not return to my lodgings, would anyone note my absence and wonder at it? Lestrade? My brother?

Unlikely. And even if they did, there would be no trail to follow. Not over water. Not without anyone else having half an idea of who I had been tracking and why. Mr. Sherlock Holmes would simply not come home, and nobody would be the wiser for it.

"Secker!" The object at my back moved, interrupting my bleak thoughts and prompting waves of torment from my injuries. "Holmes, I mean. You're alive, oh, thank Heavens."

With Wright's words, my eyes refocussed on the cramped cabin and its other carefully bound occupant. The engine of my mind started anew, cool intellect ticking along, tallying and measuring our chances, a mental clock rewound by careful consciousness and sudden hopes. Two meant for far better odds.

Wright manoeuvred in place as best he could, the motions separating us and forcing my back into a collision with the hard wooden bench. I cried out from the pain. The man at the wheel barked a one-word order to his companions in the saloon. One of them rose and picked his way back along the launch's length. He entered our cabin, fully backlit, but I recognised him all the same.

"Mr. Tobias-Henry Price. I am ever so glad to see that you were not taken by force."

He sneered and, having shut the door behind him, came and sat down on the bench across from us.

"Where is it?"

With our continued existence dependent upon

Price's ignorance, I prayed for silence from my companion. Neither he nor I made answer.

"Don't make me set Ledoux on you again, Holmes. Where is the damned deed? And you, Wright! Aren't you too much a gentleman now to let something happen to him? By my count, you're still that same snivelling coward that you were when my uncle browbeat you into stealing my life from me. Or maybe that story is just another lie. A false modesty from a false friend who cannot help but help himself to other people's things."

"Interesting words from a man who chose to abduct himself, planting a false trail to draw us into carelessness. A man who, by his own confession, stole that very deed out of the hands of the very men with whom he is now allied. You've a rather winsome way about you, Thomas Hall. Turning dire enemies into partners is no mean trick," I countered.

Price jolted towards me, fists raised. He held off the promised blows, however, and instead laughed into our faces. I had judged him rightly. Much bluster, much bravado. But the action, the true menace, that he left to his hired guns.

"It will be easy cleanup, you see." He sat back on the bench, wholly at ease as he teased his prey. "Two bodies dumped over the side in the black of night. The Channel is quite the grave for a person. Big enough for a man of your reputation, Holmes; wide enough for even your ambitions, Wright."

He looked back to me. "So you saw through it? And yet came running out into my trap. Tsk, tsk, Mr. Detective."

I smiled. "I ran after Mr. Wright. He believed the ruse. Your implications that Miss Clarke might be endangered set his stout and courageous heart to seek after the lady's well-being. It was his straight cross that I did not see."

"I would never harm Eudora, no. You've seen the ring. You, Holmes, have met her and know she is besotted with me and I with her——"

"You brute!" Wright could no longer remain silent. "You are not worthy to have her name on your lips. Even if I had the deed, I wouldn't tell you where it is. I would sooner we all die here and now than to see her under your power."

Wright a coward? No. A fool? Yes. Inwardly I groaned my annoyance that he should have spoken so passionately out of turn. Volunteer your own death, Mr. Wyat Wright. I, for one, should like to live to see tomorrow.

Price seemed taken aback by the outburst. Taken aback and alarmed.

"Hsssst!" he cautioned, kneeling down close. "Don't you dare tell me that you haven't that deed. Don't you even suggest it. Not while they can hear you."

Ah! My flicker of hope wavered in the changing, charged air between us. Price was not as in command as he would have us believe.

"It's true," I added, eyeing the man at the helm and the forward cabin with its grouping of American gunslingers. "The cane you took off Wright—Sir Edgar's famed aluminium crutch—is a replica, a clever duplicate to replace the real one which was lost some months back."

"I never thought that anything had been concealed in it until today, Price. This I swear," Wright vowed.

Stricken, Price passed a trembling hand over his mouth. His eyes, too, were trained on his dangerous companions. He spoke, "Then it is your deaths you have earned. Not mine. Sloane and the rest will simply have to listen to reason. They've seen my uncle's house. They will know its worth."

"There will be no buying your freedom from their justice, Price," I cautioned. "The fever which catches at a man and draws him to those wild lands that you were sent to oversee on your uncle's behalf? Only one thing can satisfy it: a strike of silver and gold, copper and iron. Sir Edgar's money is not the currency of your Jacks Creek Gang."

As if in confirmation of this very fact, the helmsman turned and opened the door. "Hall?"

"Everything is fine, Reece. You tell Telton and Herrera that we'll be needing some rope and weights in a few minutes." Price half rose to seat himself back on the bench. A pointed and careful distancing of himself from us, the gesture earned him a nod of the head from Reece who shut the door and turned back to his duties of directing the boat across the dark and silent waters.

"Wright will tell you how wealthy my uncle was. Every man can be bought. Every man." Price's eyes shone. "I'll claim all, pay my debts, and take Eudora off to anywhere she wishes to go, so long as it is far from England's shores."

"And how will you make your claim stand?" Wright sputtered. "Sir Edgar is dead! Nobody will believe you. They'll wait on a word from me, the Tobias-Henry Price who they know."

I added, "Even then, after the events at your uncle's home—"

"Quiet!" This time, Price made good on his threats. His fists flew, and I had two new bruises atop my old. My head fairly rang under the sudden assault, and I only barely registered Wright's lashing out with his feet in a feeble attempt at coming to my defence.

"You've lost, Price. Admit it. Even if you manage to work everything out to your advantage, Miss Clarke will never have you. Our blood, the blood of your uncle, and everyone else who fell to your Jacks Creek murderers . . . all will keep her heart from ever uniting with yours," Wright spat. "I should know, having spent many an hour in her company while you hid from the consequences of your own sins. You're so far from the man she believed she loved, you haven't a chance of keeping that woman save by force."

With that, something in Price's face twisted and then broke. Some hardened resolve snapped. He exhaled, falling back against the window as though he had been punched in the gut, and his face turned a curious waxen cast. His jaw worked emptily for several seconds while he hunted about his pockets. Connecting, his hand drew forth a small clasp-knife. Tapping the handle against his lips, Price said nothing, and then, sliding the object back into his pocket, he rose and exited the cabin.

DISASTER AT SEA

CHAPTER 20

rice relieved the man at the helm. After
passing a few words to his captain that I
could not make out, Reece ducked his head
and entered the fore cabin. Long moments passed
before Wright shimmied close to my side and bent
to speak, "What now?"

I gave no answer. My eyes were fixed upon the
floor where the edge of the opposing bench all but
disappeared into the nighttime gloom. I could swear
that some small object lay there in the deep shadows, but unable to change my position without
aggravating my innumerable lacerations, I had to
wait for the count of thirty seconds.

On cue, the three flashes of a lightship's beam
cut across the space and was gone. I whispered
back, "If we are able to get free, we've a chance at
swimming for the lightship. But that is only if we
are able to make good on it before we pass too far

by and only if the water is kindly. How are you at swimming?"

"Why don't we just take the boat ourselves? Price—he isn't looking. And the rest are up at the bow now or in the saloon."

"No. Not these men." I shook my head. "They'll be armed, and I have seen firsthand the violence that they are capable of."

"How are we to get free? My bonds are tight as can be."

I kept my eyes fixed upon that dark corner of the cabin floor. "Patience. And keep an eye on Price."

With that cryptic warning, I eased my legs over and out towards the doorway. Price had left the door open behind him, and I could feel the breeze of the nighttime air fresh and salty upon my face. I estimated we were moving at a fair clip.

An errant wave knocked hard against the hull, and the object of my attentions slid a few inches out from under the seat's edge. I clenched my teeth and ceased my careful movement forward. I was now fairly certain that the small bone-handled item was the very same knife that Price had toyed with in the moments before he had exited the cabin. I had watched him place it in his pocket. Could he really have been so careless as to drop it? I glanced his way. He stood at the wheel, his back to the captives on board.

Little by little, I manoeuvred myself so that I sat feet-first toward the doorway, sitting unsupported in my bid to place myself near where Price had crouched. Another knock of a wave against the hull, and the man at the helm turned. In the next sweeping flashes of the beacon from the nearest lightship, Price's eyes made contact with my own.

I froze, knowing that he saw my new position and the knife which, having slid further, now lay in full view of the open door. His eyes darted from me, to it, and then back again to me. He gave a curt nod before turning back to the wheel.

A shiver broke over me. One which, for all the violence it did upon my open wounds, gave me the strength I needed to lurch sideways and get my hand upon the knife handle. With a grimace, I pried it open and set to work upon the cloths which bound my hands behind my back. Bending my knees, I applied the same treatment to that which held my ankles. Wide-eyed Wright watched in silence, his face hardly even registering a flicker of emotion when I knelt and turned the knife to his bonds.

Each of us resumed some semblance of our helpless positions as Price again half turned to look in on the boat's captives. He leaned back and whispered, "Is it done?"

What is your game, Price? I narrowed my eyes and nodded assent.

Whipping around, he reached for the heavy shovel used to tend the engine and feed it coal. Another barked order from Price and a point to starboard had the men of Jacks Creek looking out over the dark water. Both Wright and I rose to our feet.

Price whipped around, taking a clumsy swing at my head. I ducked and moved forward to the double brass railing that ran along the midship gunwale. Wright filed in behind me, swearing.

I watched as Price grabbed hold of his doppelgänger's lapels and threw him hard against the steamer's smoke-stack. From the corner of my eye, I saw the rest of the Jacks Creek Gang fumble for their weapons.

"Price!" I shouted, lunging past them to slam shut the door on the forward cabin and ducking as a shot rang out. The bullet ricocheted off the aft cabin's roof. Wright was over the side of the launch and in the water in the blink of an eye.

Price turned to me then, his eyes blazing as he grabbed hold of my shoulders and shouted hard in my ear, "You'll be swimming for it! Best of luck, Detective."

The world flipped on me, and the icy water of the Channel had me in its grasp before I could so much as draw a breath. Quickly setting my eyes upon the departing launch, I saw Price raining blows upon the ship's boiler with his makeshift bludgeon. He was overcome within moments as his four American *desperados* subdued the traitor at last.

My injuries were to work against me as I struggled to stay afloat but silent within the icy waters.

"Mr. Holmes!" Wright's whispered exclamation dove at me from out of the darkness somewhere at my back. With a grunt and none-too-quiet splashing, he came upon me and, lending an arm, did his best to support us both. Concussive waves battered at our fragile buoyancy, yet each of us strove to keep the boat in sight. They were now over a hundred yards off and slowly coming to port so as to turn back around and search for their escapees. My back twinged, and I bit my lip against the impulse to cry out from the pain.

With a roar, Price shook off his attackers. His violent efforts against the craft's engine echoed over the water. A brief flash and distance-delayed report of a pistol. We were not yet in the clear. They could still find us. They could still turn 'round.

As if in confirmation of this thought, a lantern's wavering beam swept over the water. Wright swore under his breath. A hellish eternity passed while we, growing numb in that icy sea, waited for discovery. It occurred to me again that nobody—not a soul— knew where we were save for the evil men aboard that boat.

A sudden blast, a deafening, eye-searing explosion, rent the launch asunder. I could feel the rumbling report in my bones even as a fireball shot skyward, illuminating what pieces of the boat remained upon the water. There was not much left of it to see, and I gave fervent thanks for the distance that preserved us from much of the discharged fragments.

Mr. Tobias-Henry Price's sabotage of the launch's boiler had wrought revenge upon his pursuers.

"Can you swim or no?" Mr. Wright gasped his question.

My arms, my neck and shoulders, had frozen in their agony, and I discovered that I couldn't even shake my head no in answer. The frigid water was weighing on me. It had drawn the pain from my wounds, a mercy. It was a warm oblivion that awaited me. Even the burning glow of the dying launch was fast fading to inky black.

"Come on, man!" The shouted words sounded close by my ears, and the tug upon my arm barely registered.

I opened my eyes, wincing as three flashes of light cut my vision. The passing beams arced through patchy fog above our heads and were swiftly gone.

"To the boat." My words came out slurred.

The boat? The boat had sunk. Intellect would not be silenced by despair, however, and patiently waited the half minute more it would take to prove its point to me.

The three flashes returned. Hope rose in its wake. A heart's perseverance supplied the rest of my needed strength, and I managed to rasp out, "Lightship. Not a mile back and she'll have seen the explosion."

"Then we are saved."

Where Mr. Wyat Wright found the strength to swim the better part of a mile in a bitter sea, dragging me alongside him, I may never know. In any event, the men aboard the Goodwin pulled us from the treacherous waters at last.

THE DEATH OF MR. PRICE

CHAPTER 21

There was no better place for our singular little affair to end than where it had begun those two weeks prior. Number 59 Montague, with a cheering fire in the hearth and the quiet calm of London all around us. Miss Clarke and Mr. Wright sat close beside one another on my little couch while I stretched out in the cane chair opposite.

Upon making land in the small hours of Thursday morning, while dawn stretched her rosy fingers out over the Sussex countryside, Wright and I had relied upon the goodness of our rescuers who, of course, turned us over to what authorities they could find at such an hour. While Wright might have mocked my name earlier in the night, he now saw the power it commanded even this far from the city.

An early train brought us in on the heels of a

quick wire to Miss Clarke, and she met us, fresh-faced and rosy-cheeked, at the station itself. She would have flung herself at both Wright and me had propriety not demanded otherwise, I believe. Still I could sense her high spirits as we claimed a cab to take us to my lodgings at long last.

As I say, the morning found the three of us utterly exhausted, seeking comfort and safety, and not entirely eager to recount our misadventures until some time had passed. But in the end, answers and explanations must be given. It was, of course, Miss Eudora Frances Clarke who deigned to break the silence at last with a, "You need a doctor, Mr. Holmes."

Cracking open one eye, I waved off the concern. My wounds were superficial. Annoying to be certain, and sure to give me no end of trouble until they had healed, they were, for me, the smallest part of the very long evening and of little concern to me at present.

Wright nodded. "She is right, you know. I have a gentleman who I could have come 'round. Honest fellow. Member of my club who . . ."

He trailed off, noting my hooded glare.

"Miss Clarke," I began, sitting myself up at last. "You will no doubt have guessed that our harried state signifies that your case was, by no means, a successful one."

And your restraint in not asking after your own Tobias-Henry Price is admirable, I added to myself.

"Upon sending you that wire last night, I collected Mr. Wyat Wright here with the intent to bring him face to face with the real Mr. Tobias-

Henry Price whom I had taken into my custody. The men pursuing him were closing in. I had little doubt they would have discovered his whereabouts soon after I did, there being a rather telling clue in one of the London papers." I raised a hand for silence and continued, "I will not say more upon it, no. Let it suffice that I found him, and he has since been lost to those powers that had long oppressed him."

Clear-eyed at last, Miss Clarke's gaze sought my own, and she said, "Do not talk around the issue, Mr. Holmes. I can guess that Toby—Mr. Price's—illicit enterprises were the source of his troubles and so had resigned myself to such an ending. I have come to learn that Toby was not quite the gentleman I thought him to be, and you will not crush my heart with your honesty in the matter."

"Very well." I sat forward in my chair. "Mr. Tobias-Henry Price had earned the wrath of a gang of New Mexico outlaws by having shot and killed one of their company, faked his own death, and then absconded with the deed to a tract of land containing a potentially profitable mine that his uncle had claim to but that one of the outlaw's names was assigned as owner. This all occurred some half a decade back, before his returning home and resuming his correspondence with you, the childhood friend he had never forgotten.

"He wanted a future with you. That was no lie, Miss Clarke. But the past would not forgive nor would it forget. His eventual solution, as you know, was to disappear entirely. He chose to hide within Newgate's high walls."

"Shameful." Miss Clarke shook her head.

"He was running for his life. I believe that, in sparing you the warning and explanation, he hoped to shield you from any potential fallout from the events to come. Mr. Price, very likely, thought that the men who hunted him would be turned away by Sir Edgar with a handsome payout for their troubles and thus make an end to it. He would then be free to rejoin you and take up the future he had dreamed of."

"But I, kept in the dark and unable to sit still and wait for word, discovered the other Mr. Price and so sought you out, Mr. Holmes."

"Setting into motion an unfortunate chain of events, yes. For my investigation brought me into closer contact with the more curious of the mysteries, that of this public Mr. Price, and consequently made an enemy of Sir Edgar. With my involvement, the Jacks Creek Gang chose to watch and wait. You see, they hadn't bargained on there being a stranger in Price's place, just as you had not."

"And Mr. Wright?"

Flushing, Wright turned to Miss Clarke, taking her hands in his. "I can only lay some of the blame upon Sir Edgar. What began as a mere ruse to uphold his nephew's failing reputation became a role I could not easily leave—both out of fear for the old man and the fact that I rather enjoyed the rights and privileges which came from being Mr. Tobias-Henry Price. I am as guilty as your Tobias-Henry ever was. Possibly more so. And so I beg your forgiveness for the incredible lie I helped to perpetuate, though I know that may be too much to ask."

Miss Clarke extricated her hands from his touch, gently laying them in her lap. She chose her words carefully. "I believe I quite liked the man I saw, rather than the man who I thought he was." Eyes cast downward, she asked, "Mr. Holmes? What of Toby? Is he dead?"

"Tobias-Henry Price died in the explosion of a steam launch in the English Channel early this morning. And he died saving our lives. This after having orchestrated our capture so as to buy freedom for himself from the revenge of the Jacks Creek Gang."

Miss Clarke gave a choking little cry and buried her face in Mr. Wright's shoulder.

He met my gaze and asked, "One thing I do not quite follow, Mr. Holmes. You claimed that you would not, yourself, have fallen to Price's ruse. You even tried to convince me before I ran off into the night, fearful for Miss Clarke's safety. So how was it that you saw through his self-abduction?"

"The telegraph forms from my desk fell in a heap when the desk was overturned. The topmost form became the bottom, and upon picking them up, I noted that it had acquired a gentle smudging of a pencil so as to reveal the message I had writ atop it but an hour before while in Price's company. He co-opted the wording with the aim of alarming you and me enough to overlook the rest of the facts," I explained. "My error, however, came in how I phrased my answer to your question, an answer I was not given leave to fully express when your fist connected with my jaw a moment later, and you dashed off in a fit of misplaced gallantry."

"The rest of the facts, you say. What facts? I saw the same room you had but concluded the opposite."

"The window, Mr. Wright. Price was in hiding. Why open that window?" I wagged a finger. "Why else but to climb out of it and break it before, himself, leaving, thus making it appear as if his abductors came in that way. With that means of egress, he could then avoid the problem of foot-prints—or lack thereof—upon the dusty stairs. He then chose to further the idea by planting his more obvious breadcrumbs: the smashing of the water glass, and overturning of the desk and chair. He even thought to catch a thread from his jacket on the rough edge of the mantle which was, admit-tedly, a nice touch. He was no amateur, no. But he was rushed and so only half followed the steps he ought to have taken, such as taking better caution not to leave a scuff on the window sill when he exited. From there I could tell only one man had gone and nobody else had entered."

Wright gave a low whistle of appreciation. Miss Clarke had regained her poise and so signalled finality to it by adding, "Toby does not earn the credit of saving you if he was also responsible for endangering you. He was a villain responsible for the ruining of many lives."

Still, Mr. Wright had one more question in him. "And the deed?"

I flashed a quick smile. "You have my card, and

my door is always open for consultation. I believe I have some familiarity with the case, Mr. Price."

Standing, Wyat Wright offered a hand and said, "Mr. Wright, please, Mr. Holmes. Mr. Tobias-Henry Price died in a boating accident this morning. You should know. You were there."

MR. LESTRADE DEDUCES A BUNSEN BURNER

CHAPTER 22

The past two weeks had brought me a client, a case, and a handful of excursions on behalf of both. It had also provided an unlikely ally in Mr. Langdale Pike. Friday morning, however, saw a return to quietude while I waited for a visit from the police on an unrelated matter. A tricky little problem of a suspected gaol-cell poisoning, the case was not the usual sort of puzzle that had begun to send a certain Yard detective 'round to my door on a semi-regular basis. But, considering the delicacy of the investigation, an amateur hand, unconnected with the police in any formal sense, was thought best.

I had just finished a late luncheon when footsteps sounded on the stairs outside my rooms, and I hastened to usher in Mr. Lestrade of Scotland Yard.

"I take it, Mr. Holmes, that the new Bunsen is less troublesome than the old and that the predecessor has been adequately censured for the problems which it brought to its owner?"

My visitor had hardly sat down when this bizarre sentence had passed from his lips. He smiled, adding, "Singed curtains."

I looked from Mr. Lestrade to the curtains and then back, a prompt that he proceed with his explanation.

"The table with your bottles, test-tubes, and retorts stands by the window. Perilously close to the newly-charred curtains. But the burner? Stands alone upon your desk, over there. Ah, but it is not your old burner, either. It is a new one. Thus, I've both chain of evidence and motive."

"Very good, Inspector."

My compliment prompted a prideful shifting in his chair. "Well, I—"

"You're perfectly wrong, of course."

"And why not." The Yard detective laughed, throwing his hands into the air in defeat. "You were doing something wholly exotic and unusual then, I presume. Proving the efficacy of optography through some original method. Synthesizing gold from baser stuffs, perhaps."

"No, Inspector. Nothing so singular as all that. I was merely making myself familiar with the properties of aluminium and encountered a slight misfortune when the powdered metal proved considerably more flammable than anticipated."

"Aluminium?"

"Yes. Remarkably resistant to corrosion—so's much the pity for me. Non-magnetic. Lightweight. Reasonably conductive, though in that it still falls behind the more practical silver and copper. A fitting material for princely baby rattles and voyages to the moon. Dare I say, with the processes involved to isolate such a metal, your comment on alchemy would not have been far off the mark twenty years back."

Lestrade's ferret features took on the customary sternness of a Scotland Yard man as he asked, "A private inquiry?"

"At this juncture, yes." I flashed a fleeting smile and rose. "But if you hear of anything odd involving an aluminium cane, do keep me in mind, will you?"

"Odd even by your standards?" He chuckled. "That I will, Mr. Holmes."

"Thank you. As to your little matter, the anticipated communication has met with unexpected delay. Come back in two—no, three—days' time, and I'll have your answer as to whether or not Jonathan Enfield is guilty of uxoricide."

Mr. Lestrade did not budge. Instead he stretched his legs before the cold hearth, content within the cane chair. He looked me over, his sallow face crumpling into a frown of arch judgment.

"Something else?" I asked at length.

His frown deepened. "You've been using yourself far too freely, Mr. Holmes. I have a whole force to back me up if it comes to it. But you, you'd best watch yourself, Holmes. You'll have enemies in this business the longer you go at it. You can't do this all on your own."

"Thank you, I shall take that under consideration."

"I mean it." He gave a pointed look to my hands. "Injuries like that do not come from a bit of flaming metal. Ah, well, you're your own man." He rose and added, "You have my thanks, as always, Mr. Holmes. Good day."

Passing through the doorway, Lestrade collected his hat and coat and was gone.

Settling back into my seat, my eyes threatened to close in drowsy surrender to the day. Two visits from Lestrade in a week? Unheard of. I should have to ask for a raise from the Yard. Well, if I were to allow myself to be listed on their roll. I snorted and reached idly for my pipe. In leaning down and hunting about the floor for my Persian slipper—temporary home of my tobacco supply—my attentions fell upon the window with its nimbus of charred curtains.

"Well, he tries." I chuckled and lifted my pipe to my lips. Drawing my legs up onto the chair, I allowed the varied sounds of the city to crawl over me, let in via the thin walls of my apartment. Within short moments I could have told a looker-on who was at home nearby what his occupation likely was and who loitered in the street below. (The latter consisted of two boys—one honest, the other bent on mischief—and a nightman who, I believe, was planning something even less honest than the loafing youths. As to the former? Far be it from me to disclose, in print, the private doings of my neighbours.) Thus I spent the early part of my grey afternoon in idle occupation while I awaited the telegram whose absence had delayed my solution for the Yard.

Again I considered Mr. Lestrade and his increased reliance upon my expertise. We had joked, he and I, that to settle a thing he simply had to leave his residence and I to stay firmly in place within my cane chair. Clearly that was no longer the case.

The dancing veil of soporific fragrance drifting lazily upwards from my pipe settled my mind and brought my attentions back on the detective's words. Lestrade hadn't even known me to be gone. The thought that had swept over my mind while adrift in the Channel flashed brightly over my brain again. I really wouldn't be missed if something went wholly wrong while I was off on some case.

Frowning, I rose and addressed the empty hearth, "Find me one man—one!—who is familiar with violence, with death, and can come away from that familiarity unscarred, unjaded. Discover for me someone who, in the face of every dark and perilous circumstance of life, can have his faith in humanity remain unshaken; a man forever and sincerely surprised by evil's creative machinations . . . Show me such a heart, and I shall gladly let such a person into my company."

I shook my head, relighting my pipe and stretching out along my couch. "No, Lestrade. I need no partner in this nasty business of mine."

But the thought was a good one.

ACKNOWLEDGMENTS

There comes a point in the process of putting out books that you want to let the work speak for itself and remain invisibly in the background. But the work does not speak without existing, and the book which you hold in your hands would not exist were it not for the talented and lovely folks with whom I work. For them, I express my gratitude and praise. MeriLyn Oblad, Egle Zioma, Bernard Faricy, D. Lieber, T. Skov, (+ my husband who will remain incognito here - love you!), and my parents who, once upon a time, thought it a perfectly good idea to let an 8-year-old kid read the whole of Sherlock Holmes canon front and backwards, in and out, until she had nearly memorized the whole of it.

ABOUT THE AUTHOR

M. K. Wiseman has degrees in Interarts & Technology and Library & Information Studies from the University of Wisconsin-Madison. Her office, therefore, is a curious mix of storyboards and reference materials. Both help immensely in the writing of historical novels. She currently resides in Cedarburg, Wisconsin.

ALSO BY M. K. WISEMAN

Sherlock Holmes & the Ripper of Whitechapel

Bookminder trilogy:

The Bookminder

The Kithseeker

The Fatewreaker

Magical Intelligence

Forthcoming titles:

The Poison Game

House of the Golden Cog

CPSIA information can be obtained
at www.ICGtesting.com
Printed in the USA
LVHW101024240622
722036LV00020BA/149/J